Richard Farmer

An Essay on the Learning of Shakespeare

addressed to Joseph Cradock

Richard Farmer

An Essay on the Learning of Shakespeare
addressed to Joseph Cradock

ISBN/EAN: 9783337734077

Printed in Europe, USA, Canada, Australia, Japan

Cover: Foto ©Andreas Hilbeck / pixelio.de

More available books at **www.hansebooks.com**

AN
ESSAY

ON THE

LEARNING of SHAKESPEARE:

ADDRESSED TO

JOSEPH CR'ADOCK, Esq;

THE SECOND EDITION,
WITH
LARGE ADDITIONS.

BY
RICHARD FARMER, B.D.
Fellow of EMMANUEL-COLLEGE, CAMBRIDGE;
AND OF
The Society of ANTIQUARIES, LONDON.

CAMBRIDGE:
Printed by J. ARCHDEACON, Printer to the UNIVERSITY,
For J. WOODYER, in *Cambridge* ; and Sold by J. BEE-
CROFT, in Pater-noster-Row; J. DODSLEY, in Pall-
Mall ; T. CADELL, in the Strand ; and M. HINGES-
TON, near Temple Bar, *London.*

M.DCC.LXVII.

PREFACE

TO THE

SECOND EDITION.

THE AUTHOR of the following ESSAY was fol-
licitous only for the honour of *Shakefpeare* : he
hath however, in *his own* capacity, little reafon to
complain of *occafional* Criticks, or Criticks *by profiffion*.
The very FEW, who have been pleafed to controvert
any part of his Doctrine, have favoured him with
better manners, than arguments ; and claim his
thanks for a further opportunity of demonftrating
the futility of *Theoretick* reafoning againft *Matter of
Fact*. It is indeed ftrange, that any *real* Friends of
our immortal POET fhould be ftill willing to force
him into a fituation, which is not tenable: treat him
as a *learned* Man, and what fhall excufe the moft
grofs violations of Hiftory, Chronology, and Geo-
graphy ?

Οὐ πείσεις, ὐδ᾽ ἢν πείσῃς is the Motto of every
Polemick : like his Brethren at the *Amphitheatre*, he
holds it a merit to *die hard*; and will not fay, *Enough*,
though the Battle be decided. " Were it fhewn,
fays fome one, that the old Bard borrowed *all* his
allufions from *Englifh* books then publifhed, our
Effayift might have poffibly eftablifhed his Syftem."
—In

——In good time!——This had scarcely been attempted by *Peter Burman* himself, with the Library of *Shakespeare* before him.—— " Truly, as Mr. *Dogberry* says, for *mine own* part, if I were as tedious as a King, I could find in my heart to bestow it all on this Subject :" but where should I meet with a Reader ? ——When the main Pillars are taken away, the whole Building falls in course : Nothing hath been, or can be, pointed out, which is not easily removed ; or rather, which was not *virtually* removed before : a very little *Analogy* will do the business. I shall therefore have no occasion to trouble myself any further ; and may venture to call my Pamphlet, in the words of a pleasant Declaimer against *Sermons on the thirtieth of January*, " an Answer to every thing that shall hereafter be written on the Subject."

But " this method of reasoning will prove any one ignorant of the Languages, who hath written when Translations were extant." —— *Shade* of *Burgersdicius !* — does it follow, because *Shakespeare's* early life was incompatible with a course of Education — whose Contemporaries, Friends and Foes, nay, and himself likewise, agree in his want of what is usually called *Literature* — whose mistakes from equivocal Translations, and even typographical Errors, cannot possibly be accounted for otherwise, —that *Locke*, to whom not one of these circumstances is applicable, understood no *Greek ?* — I suspect, *Rollin's* Opinion of our Philosopher was not founded on this argument.

Shakespeare wanted not the Stilts of Languages to raise him above all other men. The quotation from *Lilly* in the *Taming of the Shrew*, if indeed it be his, strongly proves the extent of his reading : had he known *Terence*, he would not have quoted erroneously
from

from his *Grammar*. Every one hath met with men in common life, who, according to the language of the *Water-poet*, " got only from *Poſſum* to *Poſſet*," and yet will throw out a line occaſionally from their *Accidence* or their *Cato de Moribus* with tolerable propriety.——If, however, the old Editions be truſted in this paſſage, our Author's memory ſomewhat failed him in point of *Concord*.

The rage of *Paralleliſms* is almoſt over, and in truth nothing can be more abſurd. " THIS was ſtolen from *one* Claſſick,—THAT from *another* ;"— and had I not ſtept in to his reſcue, poor *Shakeſpeare* had been ſtript as naked of ornament, as when he firſt *held Horſes* at the door of the Playhouſe.

The late ingenious and modeſt Mr. *Dodſley* declared himſelf

" Untutor'd in the lore of *Greece* or *Rome* :"

Yet let us take a paſſage at a venture from any of his performances, and a thouſand to one, it is ſtolen. Suppoſe it be his celebrated Compliment to the *Ladies*, in one of his earlieſt pieces, *The Toy-ſhop :* " A good Wife makes the cares of the World ſit eaſy, and adds a ſweetneſs to its pleaſures ; ſhe is a Man's beſt Companion in Proſperity, and his only Friend in Adverſity ; the carefulleſt preſerver of his Health, and the kindeſt Attendant in his Sickneſs ; a faithful Adviſer in Diſtreſs, a Comforter in Affliction, and a prudent Manager in all his domeſtic Affairs."—*Plainly*, from a fragment of *Euripides* preſerved by *Stobæus*.

" Γυνὴ γὰρ ἐν κακοῖσι κ̀ νόσοις πέσει
" Ηδισόν ἐςι, δώματ' ἦν οἰκῇ καλῶς,
'Οργήν τε πραϋνᾶσα, κ̀ δυθυμίας
Ψυχὴν μεθιςᾶσ' !"——*Par.* 4to. 1623.

Malvolio

PREFACE.

Malvolio in the *Twelfth-Night* of *Shakespeare* hath fome expreffions very fimilar to *Alnafchar* in the *Arabian Tales :* which perhaps may be fufficient for *fome* Criticks to prove his acquaintance with *Arabic !*

It feems however, at laft, that " *Tafte* fhould determine the matter." This, as *Bardolph* expreffes it, is a *word of exceeding good command :* but I am willing, that the Standard itfelf be fomewhat better afcertained before it be oppofed to demonftrative Evidence. —— Upon the whole, I may confider myfelf, as the *Pioneer* of the *Commentators :* I have removed a deal of *learned Rubbifh,* and pointed out to them *Shakefpeare's* track in the ever-pleafing *Paths of Nature.* This was neceffarily a previous Inquiry ; and I hope I may affume with fome confidence, what one of the firft Criticks of the Age was pleafed to declare on reading the former Edition, that " The Queftion is *now* for ever decided."

.*. I may juft remark, left they be miftaken for *Errata,* that the word *Catherine* in the 47th page is written, according to the old Orthography, for *Catharine ;* and that the paffage in the 51ft page is copied from *Upton,* who improperly calls *Horatio* and *Marcellus* in *Hamlet,* " the *Centinels.*"

In p. 23. l. 23. for *had probably* read *might have* &c.
In p. 2. l. 11. for Effay *of,* read *on Shakefpeare.*
In p 37. l. 26. after *Henderfon,* add, *or Henryfon,* according to other Authorities.
In p. 52. at the bottom, read, *Tullius of olde age,* printed with the *boke of Frendfhipe,* by *John Tiptoft,* Earl of *Worcefter.* I believe the former was tranflated by *Wyllyam Wyrceftre,* alias *Botaner.*
In p. 84. l. 28. for *fupicion,* read *fufpicion.*

A N

E S S A Y

ON THE

LEARNING OF SHAKESPEARE:

ADDRESSED TO

JOSEPH CRADOCK, Efq;

" SHAKESPEARE, fays a Brother of the *Craft*, ᵃ
is a vaft garden of criticifm :" and certainly
no one can be favoured with more weeders *gratis*.

But how often, my dear Sir, are weeds and
flowers torn up indifcriminately?— the ravaged fpot
is re-planted in a moment, and a profufion of critical thorns thrown over it for fecurity.

" A prudent man therefore would not venture
his fingers amongft them."

ᵃ Mr. *Seward* in his Preface to *Beaumont* and *Fletcher*,
10 Vol. 8vo. 1750.

Be however in little pain for your friend, who regards himfelf fufficiently to be cautious :—yet he afferts with confidence, that no improvement can be expected, whilft the natural foil is miftaken for a hot-bed, and the Natives of the banks of *Avon* are fcientifically choked with the culture of exoticks.

Thus much for metaphor ; it is contrary to the *Statute* to fly out fo early : but who can tell, whether it may not be demonftrated by fome critick or other, that a deviation from rule is peculiarly happy in an Effay of *Shakefpeare !*

You have long known my opinion concerning the literary acquifitions of our immortal Dramatift ; and remember how I congratulated myfelf on my coincidence with the laft and beft of his Editors. I told you however, that his *fmall Latin and lefs Greek* b would ftill be litigated, and you fee very affuredly that I was not miftaken. The trumpet hath been founded againft " the darling project of reprefenting *Shakefpeare* as one of the illiterate vulgar ;" and indeed to fo good purpofe, that I would by all means recommend the performer to the army of

b This paffage of *Ben. Jonfon,* fo often quoted, is given us in the admirable preface to the late Edition, with a various reading, " fmall Latin and *no* Greek," which hath been held up to the Publick for a modern fophiftication : yet whether an error or not, it was adopted above a Century ago by *W. Towers* in a Panegyrick on *Cartwright.* His Eulogy, with more than fifty others, on this now forgotten Poet, was prefixed to the Edit. 1651.

the

the *braying Faction*, recorded by *Cervantes*. The teſtimony of his contemporaries is again diſputed; conſtant tradition is oppoſed by flimſy arguments; and nothing is heard, but confuſion and nonſenſe. One could ſcarcely imagine this a topick very likely to inflame the paſſions: it is aſſerted by *Dryden*, that " thoſe who accuſe him to have wanted learning, give him the greateſt commendation;" yet an attack upon an article of faith hath been uſually received with more temper and complacence, than the unfortunate opinion, which I am about to defend.

But let us previouſly lament with every lover of *Shakeſpeare*, that the Queſtion was not fully diſcuſſed by Mr. *Johnſon* himſelf: what he ſees intuitively, others muſt arrive at by a ſeries of proofs; and I have not time to *teach* with preciſion: be contented therefore with a few curſory obſervations, as they may happen to ariſe from the Chaos of Papers, you have ſo often laughed at, " a ſtock ſufficient to ſet up an *Editor in form*." I am convinced of the ſtrength of my cauſe, and ſuperior to any little advantage from ſophiſtical arrangements.

General poſitions without proofs will probably have no great weight on either ſide, yet it may not ſeem fair to ſuppreſs them: take them therefore as their authors occur to me, and we will afterward proceed to particulars.

The teſtimony of *Ben.* ſtands foremoſt; and

ſome

some have held it sufficient to decide the contro-
versy : in the warmest Panegyrick, that ever was
written, he apologizes[c] for what *he* supposed the only
defect in his " beloved friend,——

——————————————— Soul of the age !
Th' applause ! delight ! the wonder of our stage ! —

whose memory he honoured almost to idolatry :"
and conscious of the worth of ancient literature, like
any other man on the same occasion, he rather carries
his acquirements *above*, than *below* the truth.
" Jealousy ! cries Mr. *Upton*; People will allow
others any qualities, but those upon which they
highly value *themselves*." Yes, where there *is* a
competition, and the competitor formidable : but,
I think, this Critick himself hath scarcely set in op-
position the learning of *Shakespeare* and *Jonson*. When
a superiority is universally granted, it by no means
appears a man's literary interest to depress the re-
putation of his Antagonist.

In truth the received opinion of the pride and
malignity of *Jonson*, at least in the earlier part of
life, is absolutely groundless : at this time scarce a
play or a poem appeared without *Ben's* encomium,
from the original *Shakespeare* to the translator of *Du
Bartas*.

But *Jonson* is by no means our only authority.

[c] " *Though* thou hadst *small Latin*, &c."

Drayton

Drayton the countryman and acquaintance of *Shake-speare*, determines his excellence to the *naturall Braine* [d] only. *Digges*, a wit of the town before our Poet left the ftage, is very ftrong to the pur-pofe,

> —— " Nature only helpt him, for looke thorow
> This whole book, thou fhalt find he doth not borow
> One phrafe from Greekes, not Latines imitate,
> Nor once from vulgar Languages tranflate." [e]

Suckling oppofes his *eafier ftrain* to the *fweat of learned Jonfon*. *Denham* affures us, that all he had was from *old Mother-wit*. *His native wood-notes wild*, every one remembers to be celebrated by *Milton*. *Dryden* obferves prettily enough, that " he wanted not the fpectacles of books to read Nature." He came out of her hand, as fome one elfe expreffes it, like *Pallas* out of *Jove's* head, at full growth and mature.

The ever memorable *Hales* of *Eton*, (who, notwith-ftanding his Epithet, is, I fear, almoft forgotten,) had too great a knowledge both of *Shakefpeare* and the

[d] In his Elegie on Poets and Poefie. p. 206. Fol. 1627.

[e] From his Poem " upon Mafter *William Shakefpeare*," intended to have been prefixed, with the other of his compofition, to the Folio of 1623 ; and afterward print-ed in feveral mifcellaneous Collections : particularly the fpurious Edition of *Shakefpeare's* Poems, 1640. Some account of him may be met with in *Wood's Athenæ*.

Ancients

Ancients to allow much acquaintance between them : and urged very juftly on the part of Genius in oppo-fition to Pedantry, That "if he had not *read* the Clafficks, he had likewife not *ftolen* from them; and if any Topick was produced from a Poet of antiquity he would undertake to fhow fomewhat on the fame fubject, at leaft as well written by *Shakefpeare*."

Fuller, a diligent and equal fearcher after truth and quibbles, declares pofitively, that " his learning was very little, — *Nature* was all the *Art* ufed upon him, as *he himfelf*, if alive, would confefs." And may we not fay, he did confefs it, when he apologized for his *untutored lines* to his noble patron the Earl of *Southampton?* —this lift of witneffes might be eafily enlarged; but I flatter myfelf, I fhall ftand in no need of fuch evidence.

One of the firft and moft vehement affertors of the learning of *Shakefpeare*, was the Editor of his Poems, the well-known Mr. *Gildon*; f and his fteps

---

f Hence perhaps the *ill-ftar'd rage* between this Critick and his elder Brother, *John Dennis*, fo pathetically la-mented in the *Dunciad*. Whilft the former was perfuaded, that " the man who doubts of the Learning of *Shakefpeare*, hath none of his own:" the latter, above regarding the attack in his *private* capacity, declares with great pa-triotic vehemence, that " he who allows *Shakefpeare* had Learning, and a familiar acquaintance with the Ancients, ought to be looked upon as a detractor from the Glory of *Great Britain*." *Dennis* was expelled his College for at-tempting to ftab a man in the dark: *Pope* would have been glad of this anecdote.

were moſt punctually taken by a ſubſequent labourer in the ſame department, Dr. *Sewel.*

Mr. *Pope* ſuppoſed " little ground for the common opinion of his want of learning :" once indeed he made a proper diſtinction between *learning* and *languages,* as I would be underſtood to do in my Title-page; but unfortunately he forgot it in the courſe of his diſquiſition, and endeavoured to perſuade himſelf that *Shakeſpeare's* acquaintance with the Ancients might be actually proved by the ſame medium as *Jonſon's.*

Mr. *Theobald* is " very unwilling to allow him ſo poor a ſcholar, as many have laboured to repreſent him;" and yet is " cautious of declaring too poſitively on the other ſide the queſtion."

Dr. *Warburton* hath expoſed the weakneſs of ſome arguments from *ſuſpected* imitations; and yet offers others, which, I doubt not, he could as eaſily have refuted.

Mr. *Upton* wonders " with what kind of reaſoning any one could be ſo far impoſed upon, as to imagine that *Shakeſpeare* had no learning;" and laſhes with much zeal and ſatisfaction " the pride and pertneſs of dunces, who under ſuch a name would gladly ſhelter their own idleneſs and ignorance."

He, like the learned Knight, at every anomaly in grammar or metre,

" Hath hard words ready to ſhew why,
And tell what *Rule* he did it by."

How

How would the old Bard have been aftonifhed to have found, that he had very fkilfully given the *trochaic dimeter brachycataleftic*, COMMONLY called the *ithyphallic* meafure, to the Witches in *Macbeth!* and that now and then a halting Verfe afforded a moft beautiful inftance of the *Pes proceleufmaticus!*

" But, continues Mr. *Upton*, it was a learned age; *Roger Afcham* affures us, that Queen *Elizabeth* read more *Greek* every day, than fome *Dignitaries* of the Church did *Latin* in a whole week." This appears very probable; and a pleafant proof it is of the general learning of the times, and of *Shakefpeare* in particular. I wonder, he did not corroborate it with an extract from her injunctions to her Clergy, that " fuch as were but *mean Readers* fhould perufe over before, once or twice, the Chapters and Homilies, to the intent they might read to the better underftanding of the people."

Dr. *Grey* declares, that *Shakefpeare's* knowledge in the *Greek* and *Latin* tongues cannot *reafonably* be called in queftion. Dr. *Dodd* fuppofes it *proved*, that he was not fuch a novice in learning and antiquity as *fome people* would pretend. And to clofe the whole, for I fufpect you to be tired of quotation, Mr. *Whalley*, the ingenious Editor of *Jonfon*, hath written a piece exprefsly on this fide the queftion: perhaps from a very excufable partiality, he was willing to draw

Shake-

Shakefpeare from the field of Nature to claffick ground, where alone, he knew, his Author could poffibly cope with him.

These cricticks, and many others their coadjutors, have fuppofed themfelves able to trace *Shakefpeare* in the writings of the Ancients; and have fometimes perfuaded us of their own learning, whatever became of their Author's. Plagiarifms have been difcovered in every natural defcription and every moral fentiment. Indeed by the kind affiftance of the various *Excerpta*, *Sententiæ*, and *Flores*, this bufinefs may be effected with very little expenfe of time or fagacity; as *Addifon* hath demonftrated in his Comment on *Chevy-chace*, and *Wagftaff* on *Tom Thumb*: and I myfelf will engage to give you quotations from the elder *Englifh* writers (for to own the truth, I was once idle enough to collect fuch) which fhall carry with them at leaft an equal degree of fimilarity. But there can be no occafion of wafting any future time in this department: the world is now in poffeffion of the *Marks of Imitation*.

" *Shakefpeare* however hath frequent allufions to the *facts* and *fables* of antiquity." Granted:—and as *Mat. Prior* fays, to fave the effufion of more Chriftian ink, I will endeavour to fhew, how they came to his acquaintance.

It is notorious, that much of his *matter of fact*

B   know-

knowledge is deduced from *Plutarch:* but in what language he read him, hath yet been the queſtion. Mr. *Upton* is pretty confident of his ſkill in the Original, and corrects accordingly the *Errors of his Copyiſts* by the *Greek* ſtandard. Take a few inſtances, which will elucidate this matter ſufficiently.

In the third act of *Anthony* and *Cleopatra,* *Octavius* repreſents to his Courtiers the imperial pomp of thoſe illuſtrious lovers, and the arrangement of their dominion,

——————————————— " Unto her
He gave the 'ſtabliſhment of Egypt, made her
Of lower Syria, Cyprus, *Lydia,*
Abſolute Queen."

Read *Libya,* ſays the critick *authoritatively,* as is plain from *Plutarch,* Πρώτην μὲν ἀπέφηνε Κλεοπάτραν βασίλισσαν Αἰγύπτε ꭗ Κύπρε ꭗ ΛΙΒΥΗΣ, ꭗ κοίλης Συρίας.

This is very true : Mr. *Heath* [g] accedes to the correction, and Mr. *Johnson* admits it into the Text : but turn to the tranſlation, from the French of *Amyot,*

[g] It is extraordinary, that this Gentleman ſhould attempt ſo voluminous a work, as the *Reviſal of Shakeſpeare's Text,* when, he tells us in his Preface, " he was not ſo fortunate as to be furniſhed with either of the *Folio* Editions, much leſs any of the ancient *Quarto's:*" and even " Sir *Thomas Hanmer's* performance was known to him only by Mr. *Warburton's* repreſentation."

by

by *Thomas North*, in *Folio* 1579; [h] and you will at once fee the origin of the miftake.

" Firft of all he did eftablifh *Cleopatra* Queene of Ægypt, of Cyprus, of *Lydia*, and the lower Syria."

Again in the Fourth Act,

—————————— " My meffenger

He hath whipt with rods, dares me to perfonal combat, *Cæfar* to *Anthony*.   Let th' old Ruffian know I have many other ways to die ; mean time Laugh at his challenge."—

" What a reply is this, cries Mr. *Upton?* 'tis acknowledging he fhould fall under the unequal combat. But if we read,

· —————————— " Let th' old Ruffian know *He* hath many other ways to die ; mean time *I* laugh at his challenge." ———

We have the poignancy and the very repartee of *Cæfar* in *Plutarch*."

This correction was firft made by Sir *Thomas Hanmer*, and Mr. *Johnfon* hath received it.   Moft indifputably it is the fenfe of *Plutarch*, and given fo in the modern tranflations : but *Shakefpeare* was miffed by the ambiguity of the old one, " *Antonius* fent again

[h] I find the character of this work pretty early delineated ;

" 'Twas *Greek* at firft, that *Greek* was *Latin* made, That *Latin French*, that *French* to *Englifh* ftraid : Thus 'twixt one *Plutarch* there's more difference, Than i'th' fame *Englifhman* return'd from *France*."

to challenge *Cæsar* to fight him : *Cæsar* anfwered, That *he* had many other ways to die, than fo."

In the Third Act of *Julius Cæsar*, *Anthony* in his well-known harangue to the people, repeats a part of the Emperor's will,

> —————— " To every Roman citizen he gives,
> To every fev'ral man, feventy five drachma's ——
> Moreover he hath left you all his walks,
> His private arbours, and new-planted orchards,
> On *this* fide Tyber."——

" Our Author certainly wrote, fays Mr. *Theobald*, On *that* fide Tyber —

Trans Tiberim—prope Cæfaris hortos.
And *Plutarch*, whom *Shakefpeare* very diligently *ftudied* exprefsly declares, that he left the publick his gardens and walks, πέραν τᵁ Ποταμᵁ, *beyond* the *Tyber*."

This emendation likewife hath been adopted by the fubfequent Editors ; but hear again the old Tranflation, where *Shakefpeare's ftudy* lay, " He bequeathed unto every citizen of Rome, feventy-five drachmas a man, and he left his gardens and arbours unto the people, which he had on *this* fide of the river of Tyber." I could furnifh you with many more inftances, but thefe are as good as a thoufand.

Hence had our author his characteriftick knowledge of *Brutus* and *Anthony*, upon which much argumentation for his learning hath been founded : and

hence

hence *literatim* the Epitaph on *Timon,* which it was once prefumed, he had corrected from the blunders of the Latin verfion, by his own fuperior knowledge of the Original. i

I cannot however omit a paffage of Mr. *Pope.* " The *fpeeches* copy'd from *Plutarch* in *Coriolanus* may, I think, be as well made an inftance of the learning of *Shakefpeare,* as thofe copy'd from *Cicero* in *Catiline,* of *Ben. Jonfon's.*" Let us inquire into this matter, and tranfcribe a *fpeech* for a fpecimen. Take the famous one of *Volumnia.*

" Should we be filent and not fpeak, our raiment
And ftate of bodies would bewray what life
We've led fince thy Exile. Think with thyfelf,
How more unfortunate than all living women
Are we come hither; fince thy fight, which fhould
Make our eyes flow with joy, hearts dance with comforts,
Conftrains them weep, and fhake with fear and forrow;
Making the mother, wife, and child to fee
The fon, the hufband, and the father tearing
His Country's bowels out : and to poor we
Thy enmity's moft capital ; thou barr'ft us
Our prayers to the Gods, which is a comfort
That all but we enjoy. For how can we,
Alas ! how can we, for our Country pray,
Whereto we're bound, together with thy Victory,

i See *Theobald's* Preface to K. *Richard* 2d. 8vo. 1720.

Whereto

Whereto we're bound? Alack! or we muſt loſe
The Country, our dear nurſe; or elſe thy Perſon,
Our comfort in the Country. We muſt find
An eminent calamity, tho' we had
Our wiſh, which ſide ſhou'd win. For either thou
Muſt, as a foreign Recreant, be led
With manacles thorough our ſtreets; or elſe
Triumphantly tread on thy Country's ruin,
And bear the palm, for having bravely ſhed
Thy wife and children's blood. For myſelf, ſon,
I purpoſe not to wait on Fortune, 'till
Theſe wars determine: if I can't perſuade thee
Rather to ſhew a noble grace to both parts,
Than ſeek the end of one; thou ſhalt no ſooner
March to aſſault thy Country, than to tread
(Truſt to't, thou ſhalt not) on thy mother's womb,
That brought thee to this world."

I will now give you the old Tranſlation, which
ſhall effectually confute Mr. *Pope*: for our Author
hath done little more, than thrown the very words
of *North* into blank verſe.

" If we helde our peace (my ſonne) and determined not to ſpeake, the ſtate of our poore bodies, and
preſent ſight of our rayment, would eaſely bewray to
thee what life we haue led at home, ſince thy exile
and abode abroad. But thinke now with thy ſelfe,
howe much more unfortunately, then all the women
liuinge we are come hether, conſidering that the
ſight

fight which fhould be moft pleafaunt to all other to beholde, fpitefull fortune hath made moft fearfull to us : making my felfe to fee my fonne, and my daughter here, her hufband, befieging the walles of his natiue countrie. So as that which is the only comfort to all other in their adverfitie and miferie, to pray unto the goddes, and to call to them for aide ; is the onely thinge which plongeth us into moft deepe perplexitie. For we cannot (alas) together pray, both for victorie, for our countrie, and for fafety of thy life alfo : but a worlde of grievous curfes, yea more then any mortall enemie can heape uppon us, are forcibly wrapt up in our prayers. For the bitter foppe of moft harde choyce is offered thy wife and children, to forgoe the one of the two : either to lofe the perfone of thy felfe, or the nurfe of their natiue contrie. For my felfe (my fonne) I am determined not to tarrie, till fortune in my life time doe make an ende of this warre. For if I cannot perfuade thee, rather to doe good unto both parties, then to ouerthrowe and deftroye the one, preferring loue and nature before the malice and calamitie of warres : thou fhalt fee, my fonne, and truft unto it, thou fhalt no foner marche forward to affault thy countrie, but thy foote fhall tread upon thy mother's wombe, that brought thee firft into this world."

The length of this quotation will be excufed for

it's

it's curiofity; and it happily wants not the affiftance of a Comment. But matters may not always be fo eafily managed:—a plagiarifm from *Anacreon* hath been detected!

> " The Sun's a thief, and with his great attraction
> Robs the vaft Sea. The Moon's an arrant thief,
> And her pale fire fhe fnatches from the Sun.
> The Sea's a thief, whofe liquid furge refolves
> The Moon into falt tears. The Earth's a thief,
> That feeds and breeds by a compofture ftol'n
> From gen'ral excrements: each thing's a thief."

" This, fays Dr. *Dodd*, is a good deal in the manner of the celebrated *drinking Ode*, too well known to be inferted." Yet it may be alleged by thofe, who imagine *Shakefpeare* to have been generally able to think for himfelf, that the topicks are obvious, and their application is different.—But for argument's fake, let the Parody be granted; and " our Author, fays fome one, may be puzzled to prove, that there was a *Latin* tranflation of *Anacreon* at the time *Shakefpeare* wrote his *Timon of Athens.*" This challenge is peculiarly unhappy: for I do not at prefent recollect any *other Claffick*, (if indeed, with great deference to *Mynheer De Pauw*, *Anacreon* may be numbered amongft them) that was *originally* publifhed with *two Latin* [k] tranflations.

But

---

[k] By *Henry Stephens* and *Elias Andreas. Par.* 1554. 4to. ten years before the birth of *Shakefpeare.* The former
Verfion

But this is not all. *Puttenham* in his *Arte of Eng-lish Poefie*, 1589, quotes fome one of a " reafonable good facilitie in tranflation, who finding *certaine* of *Anacreon's* Odes very well tranflated by *Ronfard* the French poet —— comes our Minion, and tranflates the fame out of *French* into *Englifh*:" and his ftric-tures upon him evince the publication. Now this identical Ode is to be met with in *Ronfard!* and as his works are in few hands, I will take the liberty of tranfcribing it.

" La terre les eaux va boivant,
L' arbre la boit par fa racine,
La mer falee boit le vent,
Et le Soleil boit la marine.

Le Soleil eft beu de la Lune,
Tout boit foit en haut ou en bas :
Suivant cefte reigle commune,
Pourquoy donc ne boirons-nous pas?"

Edit. Fol. p. 507.

I know not, whether an obfervation or two rela-tive to our Author's acquaintance with *Homer*, be worth our inveftigation. The ingenious Mrs. *Lenox* obferves on a paffage of *Troilus and Creffida*, where

Verfion hath been afcribed without reafon to *John Dorat.* Many other Tranflators appeared before the end of the Century: and particularly the Ode in queftion was made popular by *Buchanan*, whofe pieces were foon to be met with in almoft every modern language.

C

Achilles

Achilles is roufed to battle by the death of *Patroclus*, that *Shakefpeare* muft *here* have had the *Iliad* in view, as " the old Story,[1] which in many places he hath faithfully copied, is abfolutely filent with refpect to this circumftance."

And Mr. *Upton* is pofitive that the *fweet oblivious Antidote*, inquired after by *Macbeth*, could be nothing but the *Nepenthe* defcribed in the *Odyffey*,

"Νηπευθές τ' ἄχολόν τε, κακῶν ἐπίληθον ἁπάντων."
I will not infift upon the Tranflations by *Chapman*; as the firft Editions are without date, and it may be difficult to afcertain the exact time of their publication. But the *former* circumftance might have been learned from *Alexander Barclay*;[m] and the *latter* more fully from *Spenfer*,[n] than from *Homer* himfelf.

[1] It was originally *drawn into Englifke* by *Caxton* under the name of the *Recuyel of the Hiftoryes of Troy*, from the *French* of the *ryght venerable Perfon and we fhiptallman Racul le Feure*, and *fynyfhed in the h ly citye of Colen*, the 19 day of *Septembre, the yere of our Lord G d*, a thoufand foure hundred fixty and enleuen. *Wynken de Worde* printed an Edit. Fol. 1503. and there have been feveral fubfequent ones.

[m] " Who lift thiftory of *Patroclus* to reade, &c."
Slip of Feeles. 1570. p. 21.

[n] " Nepenthe is a drinck of foueragne grace,
   Deuized by the Gods, for to aflwage
Harts grief, and bitter gall away to chace——
   In ftead thereof fweet peace and quietage
It doth eftablifh in the troubled mynd, &c."
Faerie Queene. 1596. B. 4. C. 3. St. 43.
" But

"But *Shakespeare*, perfifts Mr. *Upton*, hath fome *Greek Expreffions*." Indeed!—"We have one in *Coriolanus*,

——————————————— " It is held
That valour is the chiefeft Virtue, and
Moft dignifies the *Haver*."——

and another in *Macbeth*, where *Banquo* addreffes the *Weïrd-Sifters*,

——————————————— " My noble Partner
You greet with prefent grace, and great prediction
Of noble *Having*."——

Gr. "Εχεια.—and πρὸς τὸν "Εχοντα, to the *Haver*."

This was the common language of *Shakespeare's* time. " Lye in a water-bearer's houfe! fays Mafter *Mathew* of *Bobadil*, a Gentleman of his *Havings!*"

Thus likewife *John Davies* in his *Pleafant Defcant upon Englifh Proverbs*, printed with his *Scourge of Folly*, about 1612;

" *Do well and have well!*—neyther fo ftill:
For fome are good *Doers*, whofe *Havings* are ill."

and *Daniel* the Hiftorian ufes it frequently. *Having* feems to be fynonymous with *Behaviour* in *Gawin Douglas*º and the elder Scotch writers.

º It is very remarkable, that the Bifhop is called by his Countryman, Sir *David Lindfey*, in his *Complaint of cur Scuerane Lerdis Papingo*,

" In our *Inglifche* Rethorick the Rofe."

And *Dunbar* hath a fimilar expreffion in his beautiful Poem of *The Goldin Terge*.

Haver,

Haver, in the sense of *Possessor*, is every where met with : tho' unfortunately the πρὸς τὸν Ἔχοντα of *Sophocles*, produced as an authority for it, is suspected by *Kuster*, P as good a critick in these matters, to have absolutely a different meaning.

But what shall we say to the learning of the *Clown* in *Hamlet*, " Ay, tell me that, and *unyoke ?*" alluding to the Βϵλυτὸς of the *Greeks :* and *Homer* and his Scholiast are quoted accordingly !

If it be not sufficient to say, with Dr. *Warburton*, that the phrase might be taken from Husbandry, without much depth of reading; we may produce it from a *Dittie* of the workmen of *Dover*, preserved in the additions to *Holingshed*, p. 1546.

" My bow is broke, I would *unyoke*,
My foot is sore, I can worke no more."

An expression of my Dame *Quickly* is next fastened upon, which you may look for in vain in the modern text ; she calls some of the pretended Fairies in the *Merry Wives of Windsor*,

———— " Orphan^q Heirs of fixed Destiny."

and

P *Aristophanis* Comœdiæ undecim. Gr. & Lat. *Amst.* 1710. Fol. p. 596.
q Dr. *Warburton* corrects *Orphan* to *Ouphen*; and not without plausibility, as the word *Ouphes* occurs both before and afterward. But I fancy, in acquiescence to the vulgar doctrine, the address in this line is to a part of the *Troop,*

and how elegant is this, quoth Mr. *Upton*, suppofing the word to be ufed, as a *Grecian* would have ufed it? ὀρφανὸς ab ὀρφνὸς—acting in darknefs and obfcurity."

Mr. *Heath* affures us, that the bare mention of fuch an interpretation, is a fufficient refutation of it; and his critical word will be rather taken in *Greek* than in *Englifh*: in the fame hands therefore I will venture to leave all our author's knowledge of the *Old Comedy*, and his etymological learning in the word, *Defdemona*. ʳ

Surely poor Mr. *Upton* was very little acquainted with *Fairies*, notwithftanding his laborious ftudy of *Spenfer*. The laft authentick account of them is from our countryman *William Lilly*; ˢ and it by no means agrees with the *learned* interpretation: for the *ange-*

Troop, as Mortals by birth, but adopted by the Fairies: *Orphans*, with refpect to their *real* Parents, and now only dependant on *Deftiny* herfelf. A few lines from *Spenfer* will fufficiently illuftrate the paffage.

"" The man whom *heauens* have *ordaynd* to bee
 The fpoufe of *Britomart*, is *Arthegall*:
He wonneth in the land of *Fayeree*,
 Yet is no *Fary* borne, ne fib at all
To Elfes, but fprong of feed terreftriall,
 And whilome by falfe *Faries* ftolen away,
Whyles yet in infant cradle he did crall, &c."
      Edit. 1590. B. 3. C. 3. St. 26.

ʳ *Revifal.* p. 75. 323. & 561.

ˢ Hiftory of his Life and Times, p. 102. preferved by his Dupe, Mr. *Afhmole*.

             lical

lical Creatures appeared in his *Hurſt* wood in a *moſt illuſtrious Glory*, — " and indeed, ſays the Sage, it is not given to very many perſons to endure their *glorious aſpects.*"

The only uſe of tranſcribing theſe things, is to ſhew what abſurdities men for ever run into, when they lay down an Hypotheſis, and afterward ſeek for arguments in the ſupport of it. What elſe could induce this man, by no means a bad ſcholar, to doubt whether *Truepenny* might not be derived from Τρύπανον; and quote upon us with much parade an old Scholiaſt on *Ariſtophanes ?*— I will not ſtop to confute him : nor take any notice of two or three more Expreſſions, in which he was pleaſed to ſuppoſe ſome learned meaning or other ; all which he might have found in every Writer of the time, or ſtill more eaſily in the vulgar Tranſlation of the Bible, by conſulting the Concordance of *Alexander Cruden.*

But whence have we the Plot of *Timon,* except from the *Greek* of *Lucian ?* — The Editors and Criticks have been never at a greater loſs than in their inquiries of this ſort ; and the ſource of a Tale hath been often in vain ſought abroad, which might eaſily have been found at home : My good friend, the very ingenious Editor of the *Reliques of ancient Engliſh Poetry,* hath ſhewn our Author to have been ſometimes contented with a legendary *Ballad.*

The

The Story of the *Mifanthrope* is told in almoft every Collection of the time ; and particulary in two books, with which *Shakefpeare* was intimately acquainted ; the *Palace of Pleafure*, and the *Englifh Plutarch*. Indeed from a paffage in an old Play, called *Jack Drums Entertainment*, I conjecture that he had before made his appearance on the Stage.

Were this a proper place for fuch a difquifition, I could give you many cafes of this kind. We are fent for inftance to *Cinthio* for the Plot of *Meafure for Meafure*, and *Shakefpeare's* judgement hath been attacked for fome deviations from him in the conduct of it : when probably all he knew of the matter was from Madam *Ifabella* in the *Heptameron* of *Whetftone*. [t] *Ariofto* is continually quoted for the Fable of *Much ado about Nothing* ; but I fufpect our Poet to have been fatisfied with the *Geneura* of *Turberville*. [u] *As you like it* was *certainly borrowed*, if we believe Dr. *Grey*, and Mr. *Upton*, from the *Coke's Tale of Gamelyn* ; which by

---

[t] Lond. 4to. 1582. She *reports* in the fourth dayes exercife, the rare *Hiftorie* of *Promos and Caffandra*. A marginal note informs us, that *Whetftone* was the Author of the *Commedie* on that fubject ; which likewife had probably fallen into the hands of *Shakefpeare*.

[u] " The tale is a pretie comicall matter, and hath bin written in *Englifh* verfe fome few years paft, learnedly and with good grace, by M. *George Turberuil*." *Harrington's Ariofto*. Fol. 1591. p. 39.

the

the way was not *printed* 'till a century afterward :
when in truth the old Bard, who was no hunter of
MSS. contented himfelf folely with *Lodge's Rofalynd*
or *Euphues' Golden Legacye.* 4to. 1590. The Story
of *All's well that ends well,* or, as I fuppofe it to have
been fometimes called, *Love's labour wonne,* x is originally indeed the property of *Boccace,* y but it came
immediately to *Shakefpeare* from *Painter's Giletta* of
Narbon. z Mr. *Langbaine* could not conceive, whence
the Story of *Pericles* could be taken, " not meeting
in Hiftory with any fuch *Prince of Tyre*;" yet his le-

x See *Meres's Wits Treafury.* 1598. p. 282.

y Our ancient Poets are under greater obligations to
Boccace, than is generally imagined. Who would fufpect,
that *Chaucer* hath borrowed from an *Italian* the facetious
Tale of the *Miller of Trumpington?*
　Mr. *Dryden* obferves on the Epic performance, *Palamon
and Arcite,* a poem little inferior in his opinion to the
Iliad or the *Æneid,* that the name of it's Author is wholly
loft, and *Chaucer* is now become the Original. But he
is miftaken : this too was the work of *Boccace,* and
printed at *Ferrara* in Folio, *con il commento di Andrea
Baffi,* 1475. I have feen a copy of it, and a Tranflation
into modern *Greek,* in the noble Library of the very
learned and communicative Dr. *Afkew.*
　It is likewife to be met with in old *French,* under the
Title of *La Thefeide* de *Jean Boccace,* contenant les belles
& chaftes amours de deux jeunes Chevaliers Thebains
Arcite & Palemon.

z In the firft Vol. of the *Palace of Pleafure.* 4to.
1566.

gend

gend may be found at large in old *Gower*, under the name of *Appolynus*. [a]

Pericles is one of the Plays omitted in the later Editions, as well as the early Folio's, and not improperly; tho' it was publiſhed many years before the death of *Shakeſpeare*, with his name in the Title-page. *Aulus Gellius* informs us, that ſome Plays are aſcribed abſolutely to *Plautus*, which he only *retouched* and *poliſhed*; and this is undoubtedly the caſe with our Author likewiſe. The revival of this performance, which *Ben. Jonſon* calls *ſtale* and *mouldy*, was probably his earlieſt attempt in the Drama. I know, that another of theſe diſcarded pieces, the *Yorkſhire Tragedy*, hath been frequently called ſo; but moſt certainly it was not written by our Poet at all: nor indeed was it printed in his life-time. The Fact on which it is built, was perpetrated no ſooner than 1604: [b] much too late for ſo mean a performance from the hand of *Shakeſpeare*.

[a] *Confeſſio Amantis*, printed by *T. Berthelet*. Fol. 1532. p. 175, &c.

[b] " *William Caluerley*, of *Caluerley* in *Yorkſhire*, Eſquire, murdered two of his owne children in his owne houſe, then ſtabde his wife into the body with full intent to haue killed her, and then inſtantlie with like fury went from his houſe, to haue ſlaine his yongeſt childe at nurſe, but was preuented. Hee was preſt to death in *Yorke* the 5 of *Auguſt*. 1604." *Edm. Howes'* Continuation of *John Stowe's* Summarie. 8vo. 1607. p. 574. The Story appeared before in a 4to. Pamphlet. 1605. it is omitted in the *Folio* Chronicle. 1631.

D

Some-

Sometimes a very little matter detects a forgery. You may remember a Play called the *Double Falshood*, which Mr. *Theobald* was defirous of palming upon the world for a pofthumous one of *Shakespeare*: and I fee it is claffed as fuch in the laft Edition of the *Bodleian* Catalogue. Mr. *Pope* himfelf, after all the ftrictures of *Scriblerus*,[c] in a Letter to *Aaron Hill*, fuppofes it of that age; but a miftaken accent determines it to have been written fince the middle of the laft century.

⸻————⸻———— " This late example
Of bafe Henriquez, bleeding in me now,
From each good *Aspect* takes away my truft."

And in another place,
" You have an *Aspect*, Sir, of wondrous wifdom."

The word *Aspect*, you perceive, is here accented on the *firft* Syllable, which, I am confident, in *any* fenfe of it, was never the cafe in the time of *Shakespeare*; though it may fometimes appear to be fo, when we do not obferve a preceding *Elifion*. [d]

Some of the profeffed Imitators of our old Poets have not attended to this and many other *Minutiæ*:

---

[c] Thefe however, he affures Mr. *Hill*, were the property of Dr. *Arbuthnot*.

[d] Thus a line in *Hamlet's* defcription of the *Player*, fhould be printed as in the old Folio's,
" Tears in his eyes, diftraction in's afpéct."
agreeably to the accent in a hundred other places.

I could point out to you feveral performances in the
refpective *Styles* of *Chaucer*, *Spenfer*, and *Shakefpeare*,
which the *imitated* Bard could not poffibly have either
read or conftrued.

This very accent hath troubled the Annotators on
Milton. Dr. *Bentley* obferves it to be " a *tone* different
from the prefent ufe." Mr. *Manwaring*, in his *Treatife
of Harmony and Numbers*, very folemnly informs us,
that " this Verfe is defective both in Accent and
Quantity, B. 3. V. 266.

" His words here ended, but his meek *Afpect*
. Silent yet fpake."——
Here, fays he, a fyllable is *acuted* and *long*, whereas
it fhould be *fhort* and *graved !*"

And a ftill more extraordinary Gentleman, one
Green, who publifhed a Specimen of a *new Verfion*
of the *Paradife Loft*, into BLANK verfe, " by which
that amazing Work is brought fomewhat nearer the
Summit of Perfection," begins with correcting a
blunder in the fourth book, V. 540.

————— " The fetting Sun
. Slowly defcended, and with right *Afpect*—
Levell'd his evening rays."——

Not fo in the *New Verfion*.
" Meanwhile the fetting Sun defcending flow—
Level'd with *afpect* right his ev'ning rays."

Enough of fuch Commentators.—— The celebrated

Dr.

Dr. *Dee* had a *Spirit*, who would fometimes conde-
fcend to correct him, when peccant in *Quantity* :
and it had been kind of him to have a little affifted
the *Wights* abovementioned. ——*Milton* affected the
Antique ; but it may feem more extraordinary, that
the old Accent fhould be adopted in *Hudibras*.

After all, the *Double Falfhood* is fuperior to *Theobald*.
One paffage, and one only in the whole Play, he
pretended to have written :

——— ——— ——— " Strike up, my Mafters ;
" But touch the Strings with a religious foftnefs :
" Teach found to languifh thro' the Night's dull Ear,
" 'Till Melancholy ftart from her lazy Couch,
" And Careleffnefs grow Convert to Attention."

Thefe lines were particularly admired ; and his
vanity could not refift the opportunity of claiming
them : but his claim had been more eafily allowed to
any other part of the performance.

To whom then fhall we afcribe it ? — Somebody
hath told us, who fhould feem to be a *Noftrum-
monger* by his argument, that, let *Accents* be how
they will, it is called *an original Play of William
Shakefpeare* in the *King's Patent*, prefixed to Mr.
Theobald's Edition, 1728, and confequently there
could be no fraud in the matter. Whilft, on the contrary, the *Irifh* Laureat, Mr. *Victor*, remarks, (and
were it true, it would be certainly decifive) that the
Plot

Plot is borrowed from a Novel of *Cervantes*, not published 'till the year after *Shakefpeare's* death. But unluckily the fame Novel appears in a part of *Don Quixote*, which was printed in *Spanifh*, 1605, and in *Englifh* by *Shelton*, 1612. —— The fame reafoning however, which exculpated our Author from the *Yorkfhire Tragedy*, may be applied on the prefent occafion.

But you want *my* opinion : — and from every mark of Style and Manner, I make no doubt of afcribing it to *Shirley*. Mr. *Langbaine* informs us, that he left fome Plays in MS. — Thefe were written about the time of the *Reftoration*, when the *Accent* in queftion was more generally altered.

Perhaps the miftake arofe from an *abbreviation* of the name. Mr. *Dodfley* knew not that the Tragedy of *Andromana* was *Shirley's*, from the very fame caufe. Thus a whole ftream of Biographers tell us, that *Marfton's* Plays were printed at *London*, 1633, " by the care of *William Shakefpeare*, the famous Comedian."—Here again I fuppofe, in fome Tranfcript, the real Publifher's name, *William Sheares*, was *abbreviated*. No one hath protracted the life of *Shakefpeare* beyond 1616, except Mr. *Hume* ; who is pleafed to add a year to it, in contradiction to all manner of evidence.

Shirley is fpoken of with contempt in *Mac Flecknoe* ; but

but his Imagination is sometimes fine to an extraordinary degree. I recollect a passage in the fourth book of the *Paradise Lost*, which hath been suspected of *Imitation*, as a *prettiness* below the Genius of *Milton*: I mean, where *Uriel* glides *backward and forward* to Heaven on a *Sun-beam*. Dr. *Newton* informs us, that this might possibly be hinted by a Picture of *Annibal Carracci* in the King of *France's* Cabinet: but I am apt to believe that *Milton* had been struck with a Portrait in *Shirley*. *Fernando*, in the Comedy of the *Brothers*, 1652, describes *Jacinta* at *Vespers*:

" Her eye did seem to labour with a tear,
Which suddenly took birth, but overweigh'd
With it's own swelling, drop'd upon her bosome;
Which by reflexion of her light, appear'd
As nature meant her sorrow for an ornament:
After, her looks grew chearfull, and I saw
A smile shoot gracefull upward from her eyes,
As if they had gain'd a victory o'er grief,
And with it many *beams* twisted themselves,
Upon whose *golden threads* the *Angels* walk
To and again from Heaven." e ———

You must not think me infected with the spirit of

e *Middleton*, in an obscure Play, called, *A Game at Chesse*, hath some very pleasing lines on a similar occasion:
" Upon those lips, the sweete fresh buds of youth,
The holy dew of prayer lies like pearle,
Dropt from the opening eye-lids of the morne
Upon the bashfull Rose."———

Lauder,

Lauder, if I give you another of *Milton's* Imitations:

—————— " The Swan *with arched neck*
" Between her white wings mantling proudly, rows
" Her ftate with oary feet."— B. 7. V. 438, &c.

" The ancient Poets, fays Mr. *Richardfon*, have not hit upon this beauty; fo lavifh as they have been in their defcriptions of the *Swan*. *Homer* calls the Swan *long-necked*, δυλιχοδειρον; but how much more *pittorefque*, if he had *arched* this length of neck?"

For *this beauty* however, *Milton* was beholden to *Donne*; whofe name, I believe, at prefent is better known than his writings:

—————— " Like a Ship in her full trim,
A *Swan*, fo white that you may unto him
   Compare all whiteneffe, but himfelfe to none,
Glided along, and as he glided watch'd,
And with his *arched neck* this poore fifh catch'd."—
           Progreffe of the Soul. St. 24.

Thofe highly finifhed Landfcapes, the *Seafons*, are indeed copied from Nature: but *Thomfon* fometimes recollected the hand of his Mafter:

—————— " The ftately failing Swan
Gives out his fnowy plumage to the gale;
And arching proud his Neck, with oary feet,
Bears forward fierce, and guards his ofier Ifle,
Protective of his young." ———

                                   But

But *to return*, as we fay on other occafions. — Per-. haps the Advocates for *Shakefpeare's* knowledge of the *Latin* language may be more fuccefsful. Mr. *Gildon* takes the Van. " It is plain, that He was acquainted with the *Fables* of antiquity very. well : that fome of the Arrows of *Cupid* are pointed with Lead, and others with Gold, he found in *Ovid* ; and what he fpeaks of *Dido*, in *Virgil* : nor do I know any tranflation of thefe Poets fo ancient as *Shakefpeare's* time." The paffages on which thefe fagacious remarks are made, occur in the *Midfummer Night's Dream* ; and exhibit, we fee, a clear proof of acquaintance with the *Latin* Claflicks. But we are not anfwerable for Mr. *Gildon's* ignorance ; he might have been told of *Caxton* and *Douglas*, of *Surrey* and *Stanyhurft*, of *Phaer* and *Twyne*, of *Fleming* and *Gelding*, of *Turberville* and *Churchyard* ! but thefe *Fables* were eafily known without the help of either the originals or the tranflations. The Fate of *Dido* had been fung very early by *Gower*, *Chaucer*, and *Lydgate* ; *Marloe* had even already introduced her to the Stage : and *Cupid's* arrows appear with their characteriftick differences in *Surrey*, in *Sidney*, in *Spenfer*, and every Sonetteer of the time. Nay, their very names were exhibited long before in the *Romaunt of the Rofe* : a work, you may venture to look into, notwithftanding Mafter *Prynne* hath fo pofitively affured us, on

the

the word of *John Gerfon*, that the Author is moſt certainly damned, if he did not care for a ſerious repentance. [f]

Mr. *Whalley* argues in the ſame manner, and with the ſame ſucceſs. He thinks a paſſage in the *Tempeſt*,

———————— " High Queen of State,
Great *Juno* comes; I know her by her *Gait*."

a remarkable inſtance of *Shakeſpeare's* knowledge of ancient Poetick ſtory; and that the hint was furniſhed by the *Divûm incedo Regina* of *Virgil*. [g]

[f] Had our zealous Puritan been acquainted with the real crime of *De Mehun*, he would not have joined in the clamour againſt him. Poor *Jehan*, it ſeems, had raiſed the expectations of a Monaſtery in *France*, by the Legacy of a great Cheſt, and the weighty Contents of it; but it proved to be filled with nothing better than *Vetches*. The Friars, enraged at the ridicule and diſappointment, would not ſuffer him to have Chriſtian burial. See the Hon. Mr. *Barrington's* very learned and curious *Obſervations on the Statutes*. 4to. 1766. p. 24. From the *Annales d' Acquytayne*, *Par*. 1537.

Our Author had his full ſhare in diſtreſſing the Spirit of this reſtleſs man. " Some Play-books are grown from *Quarto* into *Folio*; which yet bear ſo good a price and ſale, that I cannot but with griefe relate it.——*Shackſpeers Plaies* are printed in the beſt Crowne-paper, far better than moſt *Bibles!*"

[g] Others would give up this paſſage for the *Vera inceſſu patuit Dea*; but I am not able to ſee any improvement in the matter: even ſuppoſing the Poet had been ſpeaking of *Juno*, and no previous Tranſlation were extant.

E

You know, honeſt *John Taylor*, the *Water-poet*, declares that *he never learned his Accidence*, and that *Latin and French* were to him *Heathen-Greek* ; yet by the help of Mr. *Whalley's* argument, I will prove him a *learned* Man, in ſpite of every thing, he may ſay to the contrary: for thus he makes a *Gallant* addreſs his *Lady*,

" Moſt ineſtimable Magazine of Beauty——in whom *the Port and Majeſty of Juno*, the Wiſdom of *Jove's* braine-bred Girle, and the Feature of *Cytherea*,[h] have their domeſtical habitation."

In the *Merchant of Venice*, we have an oath " By *two-headed Janus*;" and here, ſays Dr. *Warburton*, *Shakeſpeare* ſhews his knowledge in the Antique : and

[h] This paſſage recalls to my memory a very extraordinary faſt. A few years ago, at a great Court on the Continent, a Countryman of our's of high rank and charaſter, [Sir *C. H. W.*] exhibited with many other Candidates his complimental Epigram on the Birth-day, and carried the prize in triumph,

" O Regina orbis prima & pulcherrima : ridens
      Es Venus, incedens Juno, Minerva loquens."

Literally ſtolen from *Angerianus*,

" Tres quondam nudas vidit Priameius heros
      Luce deas ; video tres quoque luce deas.

Hoc majus ; tres uno in corpore : *Cælia ridens*
      Eſt Venus, incedens Juno, Minerva loquens."

Delitiæ Ital. Poet. by *Gruter*, under the anagrammatic Name of *Ranutius Gherus*. 1608. V. 1. p. 189.

Perhaps the *latter part* of the Epigram was met with in a whimſical book, which had it's day of Fame, *Robert Burton's Anatomy of Melancholy*. Fol. 1652. 6th Edit. p.520.

fo again does the *Water-poet*, who defcribes *Fortune*,
" Like a *Janus* with a *double-face.*"

But *Shakefpeare* hath fomewhere at *Latin Motto*,
quoth Dr. *Sewel*; and fo hath *John Taylor*, and a
whole Poem upon it into the bargain.

You perceive, my dear Sir, how vague and inde-
terminate fuch arguments muft be : for in fact this
fweet Swan of Thames, as Mr. *Pope* calls him, hath
more fcraps of *Latin*, and allufions to antiquity than
are any where to be met with in the writings of
Shakefpeare. I am forry to trouble you with trifles,
yet what muft be done, when grave men infift upon
them ?

It fhould feem to be the opinion of fome modern
criticks, that the perfonages of claffick land began only
to be known in *England* in the time of *Shakefpeare*;
or rather, that he particularly had the honour of in-
troducing them to the notice of his countrymen.

For inftance, — *Rumour painted full of tongues*, gives
us a Prologue to one of the parts of *Henry the Fourth*;
and, fays Dr. *Dodd*, *Shakefpeare* had doubtlefs a view
to either *Virgil* or *Ovid* in their defcription of *Fame*.

But why fo ? *Stephen Hawes* in his *Paftime of Pleafure* had long before exhibited her in the fame manner,

" A goodly Lady envyroned about
With *tongues* of fyre." [i] ——

[i] Cap. 1. 4to. 1555.

and fo had Sir *Thomas More* in one of his *Pageants*, ^k

" *Fame* I am called, mervayle you nothing
Though with *tonges* I am compaffed all rounde."

not to mention her elaborate Portrait by *Chaucer*, in
the *Boke of Fame*; and by *John Higgins*, one of the
Affiftants in the *Mirour for Magiftrates*, in his Legend
of King *Albanačte*.

A very liberal Writer on the *Beauties of Poetry*,
who hath been more converfant in the ancient Literature of other Countries, than his own, " cannot
but wonder, that a Poet, whofe claffiçal Images
are compofed of the fineft parts, and breath the very
fpirit of ancient Mythology, fhould pafs for being
illiterate :"

" See what a grace was feated on his brow!
Hyperion's curls : the front of *Jove* himfelf :
An eye like *Mars* to threaten and command :
A ftation like the herald *Mercury*,
New lighted on a heaven-kiffing hill."   *Hamlet.*

Illiterate is an ambiguous term: the queftion is,
whether Poetick Hiftory could be only known by an
Adept in *Languages*. It is no reflection on this ingenious Gentleman, when I fay, that I ufe on this occafion the words of a *better* Critick, who yet was not
willing to carry the *illiteracy* of our Poet *too far* : —

^k Amongft " the things, which Mayfter *More* wrote in his
youth for his paftime," prefixed to his *Workes*. 1557. Fol.
" They

" They who are in fuch aftonifhment at the *learning* of *Shakefpeare*, forget that the Pagan Imagery was familiar to all the Poets of his time ; and that abundance of this fort of learning was to be picked up from almoft every *Englifh* book, that he could take into his hands." For not to infift upon *Stephen Bateman's* Golden booke of the leaden Goddes, 1577, and feveral other laborious compilations on the fubject, all this and much more Mythology might as perfectly have been learned from the *Teftament of Crefeide*,[l] and the *Fairy Queen*,[m] as from a regular *Pantheon* or *Polymetis* himfelf.

Mr. *Upton*, not contented with *Heathen* learning, when he finds it in the text, muft neceffarily fuperadd it, when it appears to be wanting ; becaufe *Shakefpeare* moft certainly hath loft it by accident!

In *Much ado about Nothing*, Don *Pedro* fays of the infenfible *Benedict*, " He hath twice or thrice cut *Cupid's* bow-ftring, and the little *Hangman* dare not fhoot at him."

This mythology is not recollected in the Ancients, and therefore the critick hath no doubt but his Author wrote " *Henchman,—a Page, Pufio :* and *this* word feeming too hard for the Printer, he tranflated the

---

[l] Printed amongft the Works of *Chaucer*, but really written by *Robert Henderfon*.

[m] It is obfervable, that *Hyperion* is ufed by *Spenfer* with the fame error in *quantity*.

little

little Urchin into a *Hangman,* a character no way belonging to him."

But this character was not borrowed from the Ancients;—it came from the *Arcadia* of Sir *Philip Sidney:*

> " Millions of yeares this old drivell *Cupid* lives;
> While ſtill more wretch, more wicked he doth prove :,
> Till now at length that *Jove* him office gives,
> (At *Juno's* ſuite who much did *Argus* love)
> In this our world a *Hangman* for to be
> Of all thoſe fooles that will have all they ſee."
>
> B. 2. Ch. 14.

I know it may be objected on the authority of ſuch Biographers, as *Theophilus Cibber,* and the Writer of the Life of Sir *Philip,* prefixed to the modern Editions; that the *Arcadia* was not publiſhed before 1613, and conſequently too late for this imitation : but I have a Copy in my own poſſeſſion, printed for *W. Ponſonbie,* 1590, 4to. which hath eſcaped the notice of the induſtrious *Ames,* and the reſt of our typographical Antiquaries.

Thus likewiſe every word of antiquity is to be cut down to the claſſical ſtandard.

In a Note on the Prologue to *Troilus* and *Creſſida,* (which, by the way, is not met with in the *Quarto*) Mr. *Theobald* informs us, that the very *names* of the gates of *Troy,* have been barbarouſly demoliſhed by the Editors : and a deal of learned duſt he makes in

ſetting

fetting them right again ; much however to Mr.
Heath's fatisfaction. Indeed the learning is modeftly
withdrawn from the later Editions, and we are quiet-
ly inftructed to read,

" *Dardan,* and *Thymbria, Ilia, Scæa, Troian,*
And *Antenorides.*"

But had he looked into the *Troye boke* of *Lydgate,*
inftead of puzzling himfelf with *Dares Phrygius,* he
would have found the horrid demolition to have
been neither the work of *Shakefpeare* nor his Editors.

" Therto his cyte l compaffed enuyrowne
Hadde gates VI to entre into the towne :
The firfte of all l and ftrengeft eke with all,
Largeft alfo l and mofte pryncypall,
Of myghty byldyng l alone perelefs,
Was by the kynge called l *Dardanydes ;*
And in ftorye l lyke as it is founde,
Tymbria l was named the feconde ;
And the thyrde l called *Helyas,*
The fourthe gate l hyghte alfo *Cetheas ;*
The fyfthe *Trojana,* l the fyxth *Anthonydes,*
Stronge and myghty l both in werre and pes." [n]

Lond. empr. by *R. Pynfon.* 1513. Fol. B. 2. Ch. 11.

Our

[n] The *Troye Boke* was fomewhat modernized, and
reduced into regular Stanza's, about the beginning
of the laft century, under the name of the " *Life and
Death of Hector*—who fought a hundred mayne Battailes
in open field againft the *Grecians ;* wherein there were
flaine on both fides *Fourteene Hundred and Sixe Thoufand,*
Fourfcore

Our excellent friend Mr. *Hurd* hath born a noble testimony on our side of the question. " *Shakespeare,*

Fourscore and Sixe men." *Fol. no date.* This work, Dr. *Fuller* and several other criticks have erroneously quoted as the *Original*; and observe in consequence, that " if *Chaucer's Coin* were of *greater weight* for *deeper learning*, *Lydgate's* were of a more *refined standard* for *purer language*: so that one might mistake him for a modern Writer !"

Let me here make an observation for the benefit of the next Editor of *Chaucer*. Mr. *Urry*, probably misled by his predecessor, *Speght*, was determined, *Procrustes-like*, to *force* every line in the *Canterbury Tales* to the same Standard : but a precise number of Syllables was not the Object of our old Poets. *Lydgate*, after the example of his Master, very fairly acknowledges,

" Well wot I ! moche thing is wronge,
Falsely metryd ! both of short and longe."

and *Chaucer* himself was persuaded, that the *Rime* might possibly be

——————— " Somewhat agreáble,
Though some Verse faile in a Sylláble."

In short, the attention was directed to the *Cæsaral pause,* as the *Grammarians* call it ; which is carefully *marked* in every line of *Lydgate* : and *Gascoigne* in his *Certayne notes of Instruction concerning the making of Verse,* observes very truly of *Chaucer*, " Whosoeuer do peruse and well consider his workes, he shall find, that although his lines are not alwayes of one selfe same number of Syllables, yet beyng redde by one that hath understanding, the longest verse and that which hath most syllables in it, will fall to the Eare correspondent unto that which hath fewest syllables in it : and likewise that whiche hath in it fewest syllables shall be founde yet to consist of wordes that have suche naturall founde, as may seeme equall in length to a verse which hath many moe syllables of lighter accents." 4to. 1575.

says

fays this true Critick, owed the felicity of freedom
from the bondage of claſſical ſuperſtition, to the *want*
of what is called the *advantage* of a learned Education.—This, as well as a vaſt ſuperiority of Genius
hath contributed to lift this aſtoniſhing man to the
glory of being eſteemed the moſt original *thinker* and
ſpeaker, ſince the times of *Homer*." And hence in-
diſputably the amazing Variety of Style and Manner;
unknown to all other Writers : an argument of *itſelf*
ſufficient to emancipate *Shakeſpeare* from the ſuppo-
ſition of a *Claſſical training*. Yet, to be honeſt, *one*
Imitation is *faſtened* on our Poet : which hath been
inſiſted upon likewiſe by Mr. *Upton* and Mr. *Whalley*.
You remember it in the famous Speech of *Claudio*
in *Meaſure for Meaſure :*

" Ay, but to die and go we know not where ! &c."

Moſt certainly the Ideas of a " Spirit bathing in
fiery floods," of reſiding " in thrilling regions of
thick-ribbed ice," or of being " impriſoned in the
viewleſs winds," are not *original* in our Author ; but
I am not ſure, that they came from the *Platonick Hell*
of *Virgil.*° The Monks alſo had their hot and their
cold Hell, " the fyrſte is fyre that ever brenneth,

° ———— —— " Aliæ panduntur inanes
Suſpenſæ ad ventos : aliis ſub gurgite vaſto
Infeſtum eluitur ſcelus, aut exuritur igni."

F   and

and never gyveth lighte, fays an old Homily: p —
The feconde is paffyng colde, that yf a grete hylle of
fyre were caften therin, it fholde torne to yce." One
of their Legends, well remembered in the time of
Shakefpeare, gives us a Dialogue between a Bifhop
and a Soul tormented in a piece of ice, which was
brought to cure *a grete brenning heate* in his foot : q
take care you do not interpret this the *Gout*, for I
remember *M. Menage* quotes a *Canon* upon us,

> " Si quis dixerit Epifcopum PODAGRA laborare, Ana-
> thema fit."

Another tells us of the Soul of a Monk faftened
to a Rock, which the winds were to blow about for
a twelvemonth, and purge of it's Enormities. Indeed this doctrine was before now introduced into
poetick fiction, as you may fee in a Poem " where
the Lover declareth his pains to exceed far the pains
of Hell," among the many mifcellaneous ones fub-
joined to the Works of *Surrey*. Nay, a very learned
and inquifitive Brother-Antiquary, our *Greek* Pro-
feffor, hath obferved to me on the authority of *Blef-
kenius*, that this was the ancient opinion of the inha-

---

p At the ende of the *Feftynall*, drawn oute of *Legenda
aurea*. 4to. 1508. it was firft printed by *Caxton*, 1483.
" in helpe of fuch Clerkes who excufe theym for defaute of
bokes, and alfo by fymplenes of connynge."

q *On all foules daye.* p. 152.

bitants

bitants of *Iceland*;[r] who were certainly very little
read either in the *Poet* or the *Philosopher*.

After all, *Shakespeare's* curiosity might lead him to
Translations. *Gawin Douglas* really changes the *Platonick Hell* into the "punytion of Saulis in Purgatory:"
and it is observable, that when the *Ghost* informs
Hamlet of his Doom there,

: "Till the foul crimes done in his days of nature
Are *burnt and purg'd away*," ———

the Expression is very similar to the Bishop's : I will
give you his Version as concisely as I can ; "It is a
nedeful thyng to suffer panis and torment—Sum in
the wyndis, Sum under the watter, and in the fire
uthir Sum :—thus the mony Vices———

"Contrakkit in the corpis be *done away*
And purgit"———
                          Sixte Booke of Eneados. Fol. p. 191.

It seems however, that "*Shakespeare himself* in the
Tempest hath translated some expressions of *Virgil :*
witness the *O Dea certe.*" I presume, we are here
directed to the passage, where *Ferdinand* says of *Mi-
randa*, after hearing the Songs of *Ariel*,

——————— "Most sure, the Goddess
On whom these airs attend."

and so *very small Latin* is sufficient for this formidable
translation, that if it be thought any honour to our

. [r] *Islandiæ* Descript. *Lugd. Bat.* 1607. p. 46.

Poet,

Poet, I am loth to deprive him of it; but his honour is not built on such a sandy foundation. Let us turn to a *real Translater*, and examine whether the Idea might not be fully comprehended by an *English* reader; *supposing* it necessarily borrowed from *Virgil*. *Hexameters* in our own language are almost forgotten; we will quote therefore this time from *Stanyhurst:*

> " O to thee, fayre Virgin, what terme may rightly be fitted ?
>
> Thy tongue, thy visage no mortal frayltie resembleth.
> —— *No doubt, a Godesse!*"　　　　　Edit. 1583.

Gabriel Harvey desired only to be " *Epitaph'd*, the Inventor of the *English Hexameter*," and for a while every one would be *halting on Roman feet*; but the ridicule of our Fellow-Collegian *Hall*, in one of his *Satires*, and the reasoning of *Daniel*, in his *Defence of Rhyme* against *Campion*, presently reduced us to our original *Gothic*.

But to come nearer the purpose, what will you say, if I can shew you, that *Shakespeare*, when, in the favourite phrase, he had a *Latin* Poet *in his Eye*, most assuredly made use of a Translation.

Prospero in the *Tempest* begins the Address to his attendant *Spirits*,

" Ye Elves of Hills, of standing Lakes, and Groves."

This speech, Dr. *Warburton* rightly observes to be borrowed from *Medea* in *Ovid:* and " it proves, says
Mr.

Mr. *Holt*,[s] beyond contradiction, that *Shakefpeare* was perfectly acquainted with the Sentiments of the Ancients on the Subject of Inchantments." The original lines are thefe.

" Auræque, & venti, montefque, amnefque, lacufque,
Diique omnes nemorum, diique omnes noctis adefte."

It happens however, that the tranflation by *Arthur Golding*[t] is by no means literal, and *Shakefpeare* hath clofely followed it ;

" Ye Ayres and Winds ; *Ye Elves of Hills*, of Brookes,
   of Woods alone,
Of ftanding Lakes, and of the Night approche ye everych
   one."

I think it is unneceffary to purfue this any further ; efpecially as more powerful arguments await us.

In the *Merchant of Venice*, the *Jew*, as an apology for his cruelty to *Anthonio*, rehearfes many *Sympa-thies* and *Antipathies* for which *no reafon can be rendered*,

" Some love not a gaping Pig ——
And others when a *Bagpipe* fings i'th' nofe
Cannot contain their urine for *affection*."

[s] In fome Remarks on the *Tempeft*, publifhed under the quaint Title of " An attempte to refcue that aunciente Englifh Poet and Play-wrighte, Maifter *Williaume Shakefpeare*, from the many Errours, faulfely charged upon him by certaine new-fangled Wittes." *Lond.* 8vo. 1749. p. 81.
[t] His work is dedicated to the Earl of *Leicefter* in a long Epiftle in verfe, from *Berwicke*, Apr. 20. 1567.

This

This incident, Dr. *Warburton* fuppofes to be taken from a paffage in *Scaliger's Exercitations* againft *Cardan*, " Narrabo tibi jocofam Sympathiam *Reguli, Vafconis* Equitis: Is dum viveret audito *Phormingis* fono, urinam illico facere cogebatur." And, proceeds the *Doctor*, to make this jocular ftory ftill more ridiculous, *Shakefpeare*, I fuppofe, tranflated *Phorminx* by *Bagpipes*.

Here we feem fairly caught; — for *Scaliger's* work was never, as the term goes, *done into Englifh*. But luckily in an old tranflation from the *French* of *Peter Le Loier*, entitled, *A treatife of Specters, or ftraunge Sights, Vifions and Apparitions appearing fenfibly unto men*, we have this identical Story from *Scaliger:* and what is ftill more, a marginal Note gives us in all probability the very fact alluded to, as well as the word of *Shakefpeare*, " Another Gentleman of this quality liued of late in *Deuon* neere Excefter, who could not endure the playing on a *Bagpipe*." ᵘ

We may juft add, as fome obfervation hath been made upon it, that *Affection* in the fenfe of *Sympathy* was

ᵘ M. *Boyle* hath delineated the fingular character of our *fantaftical* Author. His work was originally tranflated by one *Zacharie Jones*. My Edit. is in 4to. 1605. with an anonymous Dedication to the King : the *Devonfhire* Story was therefore well known in the time of *Shakefpeare.* —— The paffage from *Scaliger* is likewife to be met with in *The Optick Glaffe of Humors*, written, I believe, by *T. Wombwell* ; and in feveral other places,

formerly

formerly *technical* ; and fo ufed by Lord *Bacon*, Sir *Kenelm Digby*, and many other Writers.

A fingle word in Queen *Catherine's* Character of *Wolfey*, in *Henry* the 8th, is brought by the *Doctor* as another argument for the learning of *Shakefpeare*.

——————————— " He was a man
. Of an unbounded Stomach, ever ranking
Himfelf with Princes ; one that by *Suggeftion*
Ty'd all the kingdom. Simony was fair play.
His own opinion was his law, i'th' prefence
He would fay untruths, and be ever double
Both in his words and meaning. He was never
But where he meant to ruin, pitiful.
His promifes were, as he then was, mighty ;
But his performance, as he now is, nothing.
Of his own body he was ill, and gave
The Clergy ill example."

The word *Suggeftion*, fays the Critick, is here ufed with great propriety, and *feeming* knowledge of the Latin tongue: and he proceeds to fettle the fenfe of it from *the late Roman writers and their gloffers.* But *Shakefpeare's* knowledge was from *Holingfbed*, whom he follows *verbatim* :

" This Cardinal was of a great ftomach, for he compted himfelf equal with princes, and by craftie *Suggeftion* got into his hands innumerable treafure: he forced little on fimonie, and was not pitifull, and
ftood

ftood affectionate in his own opinion : in open prefence he would lie and feie untruth, and was double
both in fpeech and meaning : he would promife
much and performe little : he was vicious of his
bodie, and gaue the clergie euil example." Edit.
1587. p. 922.

Perhaps after this quotation, you may not think,
that Sir *Thomas Hanmer*, who reads *Tyth'd*—inftead of *Ty'd all the kingdom*, deferves quite fo
much of Dr. *Warburton's* feverity. —— Indifputably the paffage, like every other in the Speech,
is intended to exprefs the meaning of the parallel
one in the Chronicle : it cannot therefore be credit-
ed, that any man, when the *Original* was produced,
fhould ftill chufe to defend a *cant* acceptation ; and
inform us, perhaps, *ferioufly*, that in *gaming* language,
from I know not what practice, to *tye* is to *equal !* A
fenfe of the word, as far as I have yet found, *unknown*
to our old Writers ; and, if *known*, would not furely have been ufed in *this* place by our Author.

But let us turn from conjecture to *Shakefpeare's*
authorities. *Hall*, from whom the above defcription
is copied by *Holingfhed*, is very explicit in the de-
mands of the *Cardinal :* who having infolently told
the *Lord Mayor* and *Aldermen*, " For fothe I thinke,
that *halfe* your fubftaunce were to litle," affures them
by way of comfort at the end of his harangue, that

upon

upon an average the *tythe* ſhould be ſufficient; "Sers,
ſpeake not to breake that thyng that is concluded,
for *ſome* ſhal not paie the *tenth* parte, and *ſome* more."
— And again; " Thei ſaied, the Cardinall by Viſi-
tacions, makyng of Abbottes, probates of teſtamentes,
graunting of faculties, licences, and other pollyngs
in his Courtes legantines, had made his *threaſore
egall with the kynges.*" Edit. 1548. p. 138. and 143.

*Skelton,*ˣ in his *Why come ye not to Court,* gives us,
after

ˣ His Poems are printed with the title of " Pithy,
Pleaſaunt, and Profitable Workes of Maiſter *Skelton, Poete
Laureate.*" — But, ſays Mr. *Cibber,* after ſeveral other
Writers, " how or by what Intereſt he was made *Laureat,*
or whether it was a title he aſſumed to himſelf, cannot
be determined." —— This is an error pretty generally
received, and it may be worth our while to remove it.

A facetious Author ſays ſomewhere, that a *Poet Laureat,* in the modern Idea, is a Gentleman, who hath an
annual Stipend for reminding us of the *New Year,* and
the *Birth-day :* but formerly a *Poet Laureat* was a real
Univerſity Graduate.
" *Skelton* wore the Lawrell wreath
And paſt in *ſchools* ye knoe."
ſays *Churchyarde* in the Poem prefixed to his Works. And
Maſter *Caxton* in his Preface to *The boke of Eneydos,* 1490.
hath a paſſage, which well deſerves to be quoted without abridgment : " I praye mayſter *John Skelton, late
created poete laureate in the unyverſite of Oxenforde,* to over-
ſee and correcte thys ſayd booke, and taddreſſe and ex-
powne whereas ſhall be founde faulte, to theym that
ſhall requyre it ; for hym I knowe for ſuffycyent to ex-
powne and Englyſshe every dyfficulte that is therein ;
for he hath late tranſlated the epyſtles of *Tulle,* and the
G   book

after his, rambling manner, a curious character of *Wolfey*:

—————— " By and by
He will drynke us fo dry
And fucke us fo nye
That men fhall fcantly
Hauc penny or halpennye
God faue hys noble grace
And graunt him a place
Endleffe to dwel
With the deuill of hel
For and he were there
We nead neuer feare

book of *Dyodorus Syculus,* and diverfe other workes, out of *Latyn* into *Englifhe,* not in rude and old langage, but in polyfhed and ornate termes, craftely, as he that hath redde *Vyrgyle, Ouyde, Tullyc,* and all the other noble poets and oratours, to me unknowen : and alfo he hath redde the ix mufes, and underftands their muficalle fcyences, and to whom of them eche fcyence is appropred : I fuppofe he hath dronken of *Elycons* well !"

I find, from Mr. *Baker's* MSS. that our *Laureat* was admitted *ad eundem* at *Cambridge:* " An. Dom. 1493. & Hen. 7. nono. Conceditur *Joh̄ Skelton* Poete in partibus tranfmarinis atque *Oxon.* Laureâ ornato, ut apud nos eâdem decoraretur." And afterward, " An. 150⅗ Conceditur *Joh̄ Skelton,* Poetæ Laureat. quod poffit ftare eodem gradu hic, quo ftetit *Oxoniis,* & quod poffit uti habitu fibi conceffo à Principe."

See likewife Dr. *Knight's* Life of *Colet.* p. 122. And *Recherches* fur les *Poetes couronnez,* par M. l' Abbé *du Refnel,* in the *Memoires de Litterature.* Vol. 10. *Paris.* 4to. 1736.

Of the feendes blacke
For I undertake
He wold fo brag and crake
That he wold than make
The deuils to quake
To fhudder and to fhake
Lyke a fier drake
And with a cole rake
Brufe them on a brake
And binde them to a ftake
And fet hel on fyre
At his owne defire
He is fuch a grym fyre!"   Edit. 1568.

Mr. *Upton* and fome other Criticks have thought it very *fcholar-like* in *Hamlet* to fwear the Centinels on a *Sword:* but this is for ever met with. For inftance, in the *Paffus primus* of *Pierce Plowman*,

" *Dauid* in his daies dubbed knightes,
And did hem *fwere on her fword* to ferue truth euer."

And in *Hieronymo*, the common Butt of our Author, and the Wits of the time, fays *Lorenzo* to *Pedringano*,

" Swear on this crofs, that what thou fayft is true —
But if I prove thee perjured and unjuft,
This very *fword*, whereon thou took'ft thine oath
Shall be the worker of thy Tragedy!"

We have therefore no occafion to go with Mr. *Garrick* as far as the *French* of *Brantôme* to illuftrate this

G 2   ceremony:

ceremony : [y] a *Gentleman*, who will be always allowed the *firſt Commentator* on *Shakeſpeare*, when he does
not carry us beyond *himſelf.*

Mr. *Upton* however, in the next place, produces a paſſage from *Henry the ſixth*, whence he argues it to be very
plain, that our Author had not only *read Cicero's Offices*,
but even more *critically* than many of the Editors :

————————— " This Villain here
Being Captain of a *Pinnace*, threatens more
Than *Bargulus*, the ſtrong *Illyrian* Pirate."

So the *Wight*, he obſerves with great exultation,
is named by *Cicero* in the Editions of *Shakeſpeare's*
time, " *Bargulus, Illyrius* latro ;" tho' the modern Editors have choſen to call him *Bardylis :* —
" and *thus* I found it in *two* MSS." —— And *thus* he
might have found it in *two* Tranſlations, before *Shakeſpeare* was born. *Robert Whytinton,* 1533, calls him,
" *Bargulus*, a Pirate upon the ſee of *Illiry* ;" and
Nicholas Grimald, about twenty years afterward,
" *Bargulus*, the *Illyrian* Robber." [z]

But it had been eaſy to have checked Mr. *Upton's*
exultation, by obſerving, that *Bargulus* does not appear in the *Quarto.* — Which alſo is the caſe with

[y] Mr. *Johnſon's* Edit. V. 8. p. 171.
[z] I have met with a Writer who tells us, that a Tranſlation of the *Offices* was printed by *Caxton,* in the year
1481 : but ſuch a book never exiſted. It is a miſtake for
" *Tullius of olde age*," by *John Tiptoſt,* Earl of *Worceſter.*

fome fragments of *Latin* verfes, in the different *Parts* of this *doubtful* performance.

It is fcarcely worth mentioning, that two or three more *Latin* paffages, which are met with in our Author, are immediately tranfcribed from the Story or Chronicle before him. Thus in *Henry the fifth*, whofe right to the kingdom of *France* is copioufly demonftrated by the *Archbifhop*.

——————————— " There is no bar
To make againft your Highnefs' claim to *France*,
But this which they produce from *Pharamond*:
In terram *Salicam* mulieres nè fuccedant;
No Woman fhall fucceed in *Salike* land :
Which *Salike* land the *French* unjuftly gloze
To be the realm of *France*, and *Pharamond*
The founder of this law and female bar.
Yet their own authors faithfully affirm,
That the land *Salike* lies in *Germany*,
Between the floods of *Sala* and of *Elve*, &c."

Archbifhop *Chichelie*, fays *Holingfhed*, " did much inueie againft the furmifed and falfe fained law *Salike*, which the *Frenchmen* alledge euer againft the kings of *England* in barre of their juft title to the crowne of *France*. The very words of that fuppofed law are thefe, In terram *Salicam* mulieres nè fuccedant, that is to faie, Into the *Salike* land let not women fucceed; which the *French* gloffers expound to be the realm of *France*, and that this law was made by King *Pharamond*:
whereas

whereas yet their owne authors affirme, that the land *Salike* is in *Germanie*, between the rivers of *Elbe* and *Sala*, &c." p. 545.

It hath lately been repeated from Mr. *Guthrie's* " Effay upon *Englifh* Tragedy," that the *Portrait* of *Macbeth's Wife* is copied from *Buchanan*, " whofe fpirit, as well as words, is tranflated into the Play of *Shakefpeare :* and it had fignified nothing to have pored only on *Holingfhed* for *Facts.*"——" Animus etiam, per fe ferox, prope quotidianis conviciis uxoris (quæ omnium confiliorum ei erat confcia) ftimulabatur."— This is the whole, that *Buchanan* fays of the *Lady*, and truly I fee no more *fpirit* in the *Scotch,* than in the *Englifh* Chronicler. " The wordes of the three weird Sifters alfo greatly encouraged him [to the Murder of *Duncan*], but fpecially his wife lay fore upon him to attempt the thing, as fhe that was very ambitious, brenning in unquenchable defire to beare the name of a Queene." Edit. 1577. p. 244.

This part of *Holingfhed* is an Abridgment of *Jhne Bellenden's* tranflation of the *noble clerk, Hector Boece, imprinted* at *Edingburgh,* in *Fol.* 1541. I will give the paffage as it is found there. " His wyfe impacient of lang tary (*as all wemen ar*) fpecially quhare they ar defirus of ony purpos, gaif hym gret artation to purfew the thrid weird, that fche micht be ane quene,

quene, calland hym oft tymis febyl cowart and nocht defyrus of honouris, fen he durſt not aſſailze the thing with manheid and curage, quhilk is offerit to hym be beniuolence of fortoun. Howbeit ſindry otheris hes aſſailzeit ſic thinges afore with maiſt terribyl jeopardyis, quhen thay had not ſic ſickernes to ſucceid in the end of thair laubouris as he had." p. 173.

But we can *demonſtrate*, that *Shakeſpeare* had not the Story from *Buchanan*. According to *him*, the Weïrd-Siſters ſalute *Macbeth*, " Una *Anguſiæ* Thanum, altera *Moraviæ*, tertia *Regem*."——Thane of *Angus*, and of *Murray, &c.* but according to *Holingſhed*, immediately from *Bellenden*, as it ſtands in *Shakeſpeare*, " The firſt of them ſpake and ſayde, All hayle *Makbeth* Thane of *Glammis*, — the ſecond of them ſaid, Hayle *Makbeth* Thane of *Cawder*; but the third ſayde, All hayle *Makbeth*, that hereafter ſhall be *king of Scotland.*" p. 243.

> " 1 *Witch.* All hail, *Macbeth!* Hail to thee, *Thane* of *Glamis !*
>
> 2 *Witch.* All hail, *Macbeth!* Hail to thee, Thane of *Cawdor !*
>
> 3 *Witch.* All hail, *Macbeth!* that ſhalt be *King* hereafter !"

Here too our Poet found the equivocal Predictions, on which his Hero ſo fatally depended. " He had learned of certain wyſards, how that he ought to take

take heede of *Macduffe*; —— and furely hereupon had
he put *Macduffe* to death, but a certaine witch whom
he had in great truft, had tolde, that he fhould neuer
be flain with *man borne of any woman*, nor vanquifhed
till the Wood of *Bernane* came to the Caftell of *Dun-
finane*." p. 244.   And the Scene between *Malcolm*
and *Macduff* in the fourth act is almoft literally taken
from the *Chronicle*.

Macbeth was certainly one of *Shakefpeare's* lateft
Productions, and it might poffibly have been fug-
gefted to him by a little performance on the fame
fubject at *Oxford*, before King *James*, 1605.   I will
tranfcribe my notice of it from *Wake's Rex Platonicus:*
" Fabulæ anfam dedit antiqua de Regiâ profapiâ
hiftoriola apud *Scoto-Britannos* celebrata, quæ narrat
tres olim Sibyllas occurriffe duobus *Scotiæ* proceribus,
Macbetho & Banchoni, & illum prædixiffe Regem futurum, fed Regem nullum geniturum; hunc Regem
non futurum, fed Reges geniturum multos. *Vatici-
nii veritatem rerum eventus comprobavit. Banchonis*
enim è ftirpe Potentiffimus *Jacobus* oriundus." p. 29.

A ftronger argument hath been brought from the
Plot of *Hamlet*. Dr. *Grey* and Mr. *Whalley* affure
us, that for *this, Shakefpeare muft* have read *Saxo Grammaticus* in *Latin*, for no tranflation hath been made
into any modern Language. But the truth is, he
did not take it from *Saxo* at all; a Novel called the

Hyftorie

Hyſtorie of Hamblet was his original: a fragment of which, in *black Letter*, I have been favoured with by a very curious and intelligent Gentleman, to whom the lovers of *Shakeſpeare* will ſome time or other owe great obligations.

It hath indeed been ſaid, that " IF *ſuch an hiſtory ex-iſts*, it is almoſt impoſſible that any poet unacquainted with the *Latin* language (ſuppoſing his perceptive faculties to have been ever ſo acute) could have caught the charaſteriſtical madneſs of *Hamlet*, deſcribed by *Saxo Grammaticus*, [a] ſo happily as it is delineated by *Shakeſpeare*."

Very luckily, our Fragment gives us a part of *Hamlet's* Speech to his *Mother*, which ſufficiently replies to this obſervation. — " It was not without cauſe, and juſte occaſion, that my geſtures, countenances and words ſeeme to proceed from a madman, and that I deſire to haue all men eſteeme mee wholy deprived of ſence and reaſonable underſtanding, bycauſe I am well aſſured, that he that hath made no conſcience to kill his owne brother, (accuſtomed to murthers, and allured with deſire of gouernement with-

---

[a] " Falſitatis enim (*Hamlethus*) alienus haberi cupidus, ita aſtutiam veriloquio permiſcebat, ut nec diſtis veracitas deeſſet, nec acuminis modus verorum judicio proderetur." This is quoted, as it had been before, in Mr. *Guthrie's* Eſſay on Tragedy, with a *ſmall* variation from the *Original*. See Edit. *Fol.* 1644. p. 50,

out controll in his treafons) will not fpare to faue
himfelfe with the like crueltie, in the blood, and flefh
of the loyns of his brother, by him maffacred: and
therefore it is better for me to fayne madneffe then
to ufe my right fences as nature hath beftowed them
upon me, The bright fhining clearnes therof I am
forced to hide vnder this fhadow of diffimulation, as
the fun doth hir beams vnder fome great cloud, when
the wether in fummer time ouercafteth: the face of
a mad man, fcrueth to couer my gallant countenance,
and the geftures of a fool are fit for me, to the end
that guiding my felf wifely therin I may preferue my
life for the *Danes* and the memory of my late deceafed
father, for that the defire of reuenging his death is
fo ingrauen in my heart, that if I dye not fhortly, I
hope to take fuch and fo great vengeance, that thefe
Countryes fhall for euer fpeake thereof. Neuerthe-
leffe I muft ftay the time, meanes, and occafion, left
by making ouer great haft, I be now the caufe of
of mine owne fodaine ruine and ouerthrow, and by
that meanes, end, before I beginne to effect my hearts
defire: hee that hath to doe with a wicked, difloyall,
cruell, and difcourteous man, muft vfe craft, and po-
litike inuentions, fuch as a fine witte can beft imagine,
not to difcouer his interprife: for feeing that by force
I cannot effect my defire, reafon alloweth me by diffimulation, fubtiltie, and fecret practifes to proceed
therein."

But

But to put the matter out of all queſtion, my communicative Friend above-mentioned, Mr. *Capell*, (for why ſhould I not give myſelf the credit of his name?) hath been fortunate enough to procure from the Collection of the Duke of *Newcaſtle*, a *complete* Copy of the *Hyſtorie of Hamblet*, which proves to be a tranſlation from the *French* of *Belleforeſt* ; and he tells me, that " all the chief incidents of the Play, and all the capital Characters are there in *embryo*, after a rude and barbarous manner : ſentiments indeed there are none, that *Shakeſpeare* could borrow ; nor any expreſſion but *one*, which is, where *Hamlet* kills *Polonius* behind the arras : in doing which he is made to cry out, as in the Play, " *a rat, a rat !*"——So much for *Saxo Grammaticus !*

It is ſcarcely conceivable, how induſtriouſly the puritanical Zeal of the laſt age exerted itſelf in deſtroying, amongſt better things, the innocent amuſements of the former. Numberleſs *Tales* and *Poems* are alluded to in old Books, which are now perhaps no where to be found. Mr. *Capell* informs me, (and he is in theſe matters, the moſt able of all men to give information) that our Author appears to have been beholden to ſome *Novels*, which he hath yet only ſeen in *French* or *Italian :* but he adds, " to ſay they are not in ſome *Engliſh* dreſs, profaic or metrical, and perhaps with circumſtances nearer to his ſtories, is what I will not take upon me to do : nor indeed is it what I believe; but rather the contrary, and that time and accident will bring fome of them to light, if not all."———`

W. Painter, at the conclufion of the fecond *Tome* of his *Palace of Pleafure*, 1567, *advertifes* the Reader, " bicaufe fodaynly (contrary to expectation) this Volume is rifen to greater heape of leaues, I doe omit for this prefent time *fundry Nouels* of mery devife, referuing the fame to be joyned with the reft of an other part, wherein fhall fuccede the remnant of *Bandello*, fpecially futch (fuffrable) as the learned French man *François de Belleforreft* hath felected, and the choyfeft done in the *Italian*. Some alfo out of *Erizzo, Ser Giouanni Florentino, Parabofco, Cynthio, Straparole, Sanfouino*, and the beft liked out of the Queene of *Nauarre*, and other Authors. Take thefe in good part, with thofe that haue and fhall come forth."——— But I am not able to find, that a *third Tome* was ever publifhed : and it is very probable, that the Intereft of his Bookfellers, and more efpecially the prevailing Mode of the time, might lead him afterward to print his *fundry Novels* feparately. If this were the cafe, it is no wonder, that fuch *fugitive Pieces* are recovered with difficulty ; when the *two Tomes*, which *Tom. Rawlinfon* would have called *jufta Volumina*, are almoft annihilated. Mr. *Ames*, who

who fearched after books of this fort with the ut-
moft avidity, moft certainly had not feen them,
when he publifhed his *Typographical Antiquities*; as
appears from his blunders about them: and poffibly
I myfelf might have remained in the fame predica-
ment, had I not been favoured with a Copy by my
generous Friend, Mr. *Lort*.

Mr. *Colman*, in the Preface to his elegant Tranflation of *Terence*, hath offered fome arguments for the
Learning of *Shakefpeare*, which have been retailed
with much confidence, fince the appearance of Mr.
Johnfon's Edition.

" Befides the refemblance of particular paffages
fcattered up and down in different plays, it is well
known, that the *Comedy of Errors* is in great meafure
founded on the *Menæchmi* of *Plautus*; but I do not
recollect ever to have feen it obferved, that the difguife of the *Pedant* in the *Taming of the Shrew*, and
his affuming the name and character of *Vincentio*,
feem to be evidently taken from the difguife of the
Sycophanta in the *Trinummus* of the faid Author; [b] and
there

[b] This obfervation of Mr. *Colman* is quoted by his very
ingenious Colleague, Mr. *Thornton*, in his Tranflation of
this Play: who further remarks, in another part of it,
that a paffage in *Romeo and Juliet*, where *Shakefpeare* fpeaks
of the *contradiction* in the nature of *Love*, is very much in
the manner of his Author:

" Amor — mores hominum moros & morofos efficit.
Minus

there is a quotation from the *Eunuch* of *Terence* also, so familiarly introduced into the Dialogue of the
Taming

Minus placet quod fuadetur, quod difuadetur placet.
Quom inopia'ft, cupias, quando ejus copia'ft, tum non velis. &c.''

Which he tranflates with eafe and elegance,

———————— '' Love makes a man a fool,
Hard to be pleas'd. —— What you'd perfuade him to,
He likes not, and embraces that, from which
You would diffuade him. — What there is a lack of,
That will he covet ; —— when 'tis in his power,
He'll none on't.'' ——   *Act* 3. *Scene* 3.

Let us now turn to the paffage in *Shakespeare* :

—— '' O brawling Love ! O loving hate ! ——
O heavy lightnefs ! ferious vanity !
Mif-fhapen Chaos of well-feeming forms !
Feather of lead, bright fmoke, cold fire, fick health !
Still-waking Sleep ! that is not what it is !''

Shakespeare, I am fure, in the opinion of Mr. *Thornton*, did not want a *Plautus* to teach him the workings of Nature ; nor are his *Parallelifms* produced with any fuch implication : but, I fuppofe, a peculiarity appears here in the manner of expreffion, which however was extremely the humour of the Age. Every *Sonetteer* characterifes *Love* by contrarieties. *Watfon* begins one of his *Canzonets*,

'' Love is a fowre delight, a fugred griefe
A living death, an euer-dying life, &c.''

Turberville makes *Reafon* harangue againft it in the fame manner,

'' A fierie Froft, a Flame that frozen is with Ife !
A heavie Burden light to beare ! a Vertue fraught with Vice ! &c.''

Immediately from the *Romaunt of the Rofe*,

'' Loue it is an hatefull pees
A free acquitaunce without reles —

            An

Taming of the Shrew, that I think it puts the queſtion of *Shakeſpeare's* having read the Roman Comick Poets in the *original* language out of all doubt,

Redime te captum, quam queas, minimo."

With reſpect to *reſemblances*, I ſhall not trouble you any further. — That the *Comedy of Errors* is founded on the *Menæchmi*, it is notorious : nor is it leſs ſo, that a Tranſlation of it by W. W. perhaps *William Warner*, the Author of *Albions England*, was extant in the time of *Shakeſpeare* ;^c tho' Mr. *Upton*, and

An heavie burthen light to beare
A wicked wawe awaie to weare :
And health full of maladie
And charitie full of envie —
A laughter that is weping aie
Reſt that trauaileth night and daie, &c."

This kind of *Antitheſis* was very much the taſte of the *Provençal* and *Italian* Poets ; perhaps it might be hinted by the Ode of *Sappho* preſerved by *Longinus : Petrarch* is full of it,

" Pace non trovo, & non hó da far guerra,
Et temo, & ſpero, & ardo, & ſon un ghiaccio,
Et volo ſopra'l cielo, & ghiaccio in terra,
Et nulla ſtringo, & tuttol mondo abbraccio. &c."

Sonetto 105.

Sir *Thomas Wyat* gives a tranſlation of this Sonnet, without any notice of the *Original*, under the title of " Deſcription of the contrarious paſſions in a Louer." Amongſt the *Songes and Sonettes*, by the Earle of *Surrey*, and Others. 1574.

^c It was publiſhed in 4to. 1595. The Printer of *Langbaine*, p. 524. hath accidently given the date, 1515, which

and some other advocates for his learning, have cautiously dropt the mention of it. Besides this, (if indeed it were different) in the *Gesta Grayorum*, the Christmas Revels of the *Gray's-Inn* Gentlemen, 1594, " a *Comedy of Errors* like to *Plautus* his *Menechmus* was played by the Players." And the same hath been suspected to be the Subject of the *goodlie Comedie of Plautus* acted at *Greenwich* before the King and Queen in 1520 ; as we learn from *Hall* and *Holingshed:* — *Riccoboni* highly compliments the *English* on opening their stage so well; but unfortunately, *Cavendish* in his Life of *Wolsey*, calls it, an *excellent Interlude in Latine.* About the same time it was exhibited in *German* at *Nuremburgh*, by the celebrated *Hanssach* the *Shoemaker.*

" But a character in the *Taming of the Shrew* is borrowed from the *Trinummus*, and no translation of *that* was extant."

Mr. *Colman* indeed hath been better employ'd : but if he had met with an old Comedy, called *Supposes*, translated from *Ariosto* by *George Gascoigne*, [d] he certainly

which hath been copied implicitly by *Gildon, Theobald, Cooke*, and several others. *Warner* is now almost forgotten, yet the old Criticks esteemed him one of " our chiefe heroical *Makers.*"— *Meres* informs us, that he had " heard him termed of the best wits of both our Universities, our *English Homer.*"

[d] His works were first collected under the singular title of " A hundreth sundrie Flowres bounde up in one small Poesie.

tainly would not have appealed to *Plautus*. Thence *Shakefpeare* borrowed this part of the Plot, (as well as fome of the phrafeology) though *Theobald* pronounces it his own invention: there likewife he found the quaint name of *Petruchio*. My young Mafter and his Man exchange habits and characters, and perfuade a *Scenæfe*, as he is called, to perfonate the *Father*, exactly as in the *Taming of the Shrew*, by the pretended danger of his coming from *Sienna* to *Ferrara*, contrary to the order of the government.

Still, *Shakefpeare* quotes a line from the *Eunuch* of *Terence*: by memory too, and what is more, " purpofely alters it, in order to bring the fenfe within the compafs of one line."——This remark was previous to Mr. *Johnfon's*; or indifputably it would not have been made at all.—— " Our Author had this line from *Lilly*; which I mention that it may not be brought as an argument of his learning."

But how, cries an unprovoked Antagonift, can you take upon you to fay, that he had it from *Lilly*,

Poefie. Gathered partly (by tranflation) in the fyne outlandifh Gardins of *Euripides, Ouid, Petrarke, Ariofto*, and others: and partly by inuention, out of our owne fruitefull Orchardes in *Englande*: yelding fundrie fweete fauours of Tragical, Comical, and Morall Difcourfes, bothe pleafaunt and profitable to the well fmellyng nofes of learned Readers." *Black Letter*. 4to. no date.

and not from *Terence?* [e] I will anfwer for Mr. *John-fon*, who is above anfwering for himfelf. — Becaufe it is quoted as it appears in the *Grammarian*, and not as it appears in the *Poet.* — And thus we have done with the *purpofed* alteration. *Udall* likewife in his " *Floures for Latin fpeaking*, gathered oute of *Terence*, 1560," reduces the paffage to a fingle line, and fub-joins a Tranflation.

We have hitherto fuppofed *Shakefpeare* the Author of the *Taming of the Shrew*, but his property in it is extremely difputable. I will give you my opinion, and the reafons on which it is founded. I fuppofe then the prefent Play not *originally* the work of *Shake-fpeare*, but reftored by him to the Stage, with the whole *Induction* of the *Tinker*, and fome other occa-fional improvements; efpecially in the Character of *Petruchio*. It is very obvious, that the *Induction* and the *Play* were either the works of different hands, or written at a great interval of time: the former is in our Author's *beft* manner, and the greater part of the *latter* in his *worft*, or even below it. Dr. *Warburton* declares it to be *certainly* fpurious: and without doubt, *fuppofing* it to have been written by *Shakefpeare*, it muft have been one of his *earlieft* productions; yet it is not mentioned in the Lift of his Works by *Meres* in 1598.

[e] *W. Kenrick's* Review of Dr. *Johnfon's* Edit. of *Shake-fpeare.* 1765. 8vo. p. 105.

I

I have met with a facetious piece of Sir *John Har-rington*, printed in 1596, (and poſſibly there may be an earlier Edition) called, *The Metamorphoſis of Ajax*, where I ſuſpect an alluſion to the old Play; " Read the *booke* of *Taming a Shrew*, which hath made a number of us ſo perfect, that *now* every one can rule a Shrew' in our Countrey, ſave he that hath hir."
—I am aware, a *modern* Linguiſt may object, that the word *Book* does not at preſent ſeem *dramatick*, but it was once almoſt *technically* ſo : *Goſſon* in his Schoole of Abuſe, contayning a pleaſaunt inuective againſt *Poets, Pipers, Players, Jeſters*, and ſuch like *Cater-pillars* of a Common-wealth, 1579, mentions " twoo proſe *Bookes* plaied at the *Belſauage* ;" and *Hearne* tells us in a Note at the end of *William of Worceſter*, that he had ſeen a MS. in the nature of a *Play* or *In-terlude*, intitled, the *Booke* of Sir *Thomas Moore*." [f]

And

f I know indeed, there is extant a very old Poem, in *black Letter*, to which it might have been ſuppoſed Sir *John Harrington* alluded, had he not ſpoken of the Diſ-covery as a *new* one, and recommended it as worthy the notice of his Countrymen : I am perſuaded the method in the old Bard will not be thought *either*. At the end of the ſixth Volume of *Leland's Itinerary*, we are *favoured* by Mr. *Hearne* with a *Macaronic* Poem on a Battle at *Ox-ford* between the Scholars and the Townſmen : on a line of which,
  " Invadunt aulas *bycheſon cum forth* geminantes,"
our Commentator very wiſely and gravely remarks :
" *Bycheſon*, id eſt, *Son* of a *Byche*, ut è Codice *Rawlinſo-*

niano

And in fact, there is such an old *anonymous* Play in
Mr. *Pope's* Lift. " A pleasant conceited Hiftory,
called, *The Taming of a Shrew* — fundry times acted
by the Earl of *Pembroke* his Servants." Which feems
to have been republifhed by the Remains of that Company in 1607, when *Shakefpeare's* copy appeared at
the *Black-Friars* or the *Globe*. — Nor let this feem
derogatory from the character of our Poet. There is
no reafon to believe, that he wanted to claim the
Play as his own ; it was not even printed 'till fome

niano edidi. Eo nempe modo quo et olim *Whorfon* dixerunt
pro *Son of a Whore*. Exempla habemus cum alibi tum in
libello quodam lepido & antiquo (inter Codices *Seldenia-
ros* in Bibl. *Bodl.*) qui infcribitur : *The Wife lapped in
Morels Skyn : or the Taming of a Shrew*. Ubi pag. 36.
fic legimus :
" They wreftled togyther thus they two
    So long that the clothes afunder went.
And to the ground he threwe her tho,
    That cleane from the backe her fmock he rent.
In every hand a rod he gate,
    And layd upon her a right good pace :
Afking of her what game was that,
    And fhe cried out, *Herefen*, alas, alas."
Et pag. 42.
Come downe now in this feller fo deepe,
    And Morels fkin there fhall you fee :
With many a rod that hath made me to weepe,
    When the blood ranne downe faft by my knee.
The Mother this beheld, and cryed out, alas :
    And ran out of the feller as fhe had been wood.
She came to the table where the company was,
    And fayd out, *Horefon*, I will fee thy harte blood."

                                                        years

years after his death: but he merely revived it on his Stage as a *Manager*.——*Ravenscroft* assures us, that this was really the case with *Titus Andronicus*; which, it may be observed, hath not *Shakespeare's* name on the Title-page of the only Edition publish-ed in his life-time. Indeed, from every internal mark, I have not the least doubt but this *horrible* Piece was originally written by the Author of the *Lines* thrown into the mouth of the *Player* in *Hamlet*, and of the *Tragedy of Locrine :* which likewise from some assist-ance perhaps given to his Friend, hath been unjust-ly and ignorantly charged upon *Shakespeare*.

But the *sheet-anchor* holds fast : *Shakespeare* himself hath left some Translations from *Ovid*. The Epistles, says One, of *Paris* and *Helen* give a sufficient proof of his acquaintance with *that* poet; and it may be concluded, says Another, that he was a competent judge of *other* Authors, who wrote in the same lan-guage.

This hath been the universal cry, from Mr. *Pope* himself to the Criticks of yesterday. Possibly, how-ever, the Gentlemen will hesitate a moment, if we tell them, that *Shakespeare* was *not* the Author of these Translations. Let them turn to a forgotten book, by *Thomas Heywood*, called *Britaines Troy*, printed by *W. Jaggard* in 1609, *Fol.* and they will find these identical Epistles, " which being so
                                                    pertinent

pertinent to our Hiftorie, fays *Heywood, I* thought-neceffarie to tranflate."—How then came they afcribed to *Shakefpeare?* We will tell them that likewife. The fame voluminous Writer publifhed an *Apology for Actors,* 4to. 1612, and in an Appendix directed to his new Printer *Nic. Okes,* he accufes his old One, *Jaggard,* of "taking the two Epiftles of *Paris* to *Helen,* and *Helen* to *Paris,* and printing them in a lefs volume under the name of *Another :* — but *he* was much offended with Mafter *Jaggard,* that altogether unknowne to him, he had prefumed to make fo bold with his Name." ᵍ In the fame work of *Heywood* are all the other Tranflations, which have been printed in the modern Editions of the Poems of *Shakefpeare.*

You now hope for land: We have feen through little matters, but what muft be done with a whole book?—In 1751, was reprinted "A compendious or briefe examination of certayne ordinary complaints of diuers of our Countrymen in thefe our days: which although they are in fome parte unjuft and friuolous, yet are they all by way of Dialogue

ᵍ It may feem little matter of wonder, that the name of *Shakefpeare* fhould be borrowed for the benefit of the Bookfeller; and by the way, as probably for a *Play* as a *Poem :* but modern Criticks may be furprifed perhaps at the complaint of *John Hall,* that "certayne Chapters of the *Proverbes,* tranflated by him into *Englifh* metre, 1550, had before been untruely *entituled* to be the doyngs of Mayfter *Thomas Sternhold.*"

throughly

throughly debated and difcuffed by *William Shakefpeare*, Gentleman." 8vo.

This extraordinary piece was originally publifhed
in 4to, 1581, and dedicated by the Author, " To
the moft vertuous and learned Lady, his moft deare
and foveraigne Princeffe, *Elizabeth*; being inforced
by her Majefties late and fingular clemency in par-
doning certayne his unduetifull mifdemeanour." And
by the modern Editors, to the late King; as " a
Treatife compofed by the moft extenfive and fertile
Genius, that ever any age or nation produced."

Here we join iffue with the Writers of that excellent, tho' very unequal work, the *Biographia Bri-
tannica :* ʰ if, fay they, this piece could be written by
our

ʰ I muft however correct a remark in the *Life* of *Spenfer*,
which is impotently levelled at the firft Criticks of the
age. It is obferved from the correfpondence of *Spenfer*
and *Gabriel Harvey*, that the Plan of the *Fairy Queen* was
laid, and part of it executed in 1580, *three* years before
the *Gierufalemme Liberata* was printed : " hence appears the
impertinence of all the apologies for his choice of *Ariofto's*
manner in preference to *Taffo's !*"

But the fact is not true with refpect to *Taffo*. *Manfo* and
Niceron inform us, that his Poem was publifhed, though
imperfectly, in 1574 ; and I myfelf can affure the Bio-
grapher, that I have met with at leaft *fix* other Editions,
preceding his date for it's firft publication. I fufpect,
that *Baillet* is accountable for this miftake : who in the
Jugemens des Savans, Tom. 3. p. 399. mentions no Edition previous to the 4to. *Venice*, 1583.

It is a queftion of long ftanding, whether a part of the

Fairy

our Poet, it would be abfolutely decifive in the dif-
pute about his learning; for many quotations appear in it from the *Greek* and *Latin* Clafficks.

The concurring circumftances of the *Name*, and the
Mifdemeanor, which is fuppofed to be the old Story
of *Deer-ftealing*, feem fairly to challenge our Poet
for the Author : but they hefitate. — His claim may
appear to be confuted by the date 1581, when *Shakefpeare* was only *Seventeen*, and the *long* experience,

Fairy Queen hath been *loft*, or whether the work was left
unfinifhed : which may effectually be anfwered by a fingle
quotation. *William Browne* publifhed fome Poems in *Fol.*
1616, under the name of *Britannia's Paftorals*, "efteemed
then, fays *Wood*, to be written in a fublime ftrain, and
for fubject *amorous* and *very pleafing*."——In one of which,
Book 2. *Song* 1. he thus fpeaks of *Spenfer :*
 " He fung th' heroicke Knights of Faiery land
In lines fo elegant, of fuch command,
That had the *Thracian* plaid but halfe fo well,
He had not left *Eurydice* in hell.
But *e're he ended his melodious Song*,
An hoft of *Angels* flew the clouds among,
And rapt this Swan from his attentive mates,
To make him one of their affociates
In heauens faire Quire : where now he fings the praife
Of him that is the *Firft and Laft of Dayes.*"

It appears, that *Browne* was intimate with *Drayton*,
Jonfon, and *Selden*, by their poems prefixed to his Book :
he had therefore good opportunities of being acquainted
with the fact abovementioned. Many of his Poems re-
main in MS. We have in our Library at *Emmanuel* a
Mafque of his, prefented at the Inner Temple, *Jan.* 13.
1614. The fubject is the Story of *Ulyffes and Circe.*

which

which the Writer talks of. — But I will not keep you in fufpenfe: the book was *not* written by *Shakefpeare.*

Strype, in his *Annals,* calls the Author SOME *learned Man,* and this gave me the firft fufpicion. I knew very well, that honeft *John* (to ufe the language of Sir *Thomas Bodley*) did not wafte his time with fuch *baggage books* as *Plays* and *Poems*; yet I muft fuppofe, that he had *heard* of the name of *Shakefpeare.* After a while I met with the original Edition. Here in the Title-page, and at the end of the Dedication, appear only the Initials, W. S. Gent. and prefently I was informed by *Anthony Wood,* that the book in queftion was written, not by *William Shakefpeare,* but by *William Stafford,* Gentleman: [i] which at once accounted for the *Mifdemeanour* in the Dedication. For *Stafford* had been concerned at that time, and was indeed afterward, as *Camden* and the other Annalifts inform us, with fome of the confpirators againft *Elizabeth* ; which he properly calls his *unduetifull* behaviour.

I hope by this time, that any One open to conviction may be nearly fatisfied; and I will promife to give you on this head very little more trouble.

[i] *Fafti.* 2d Edit. V. 1. 208. — It will be feen on turning to the former Edition, that the latter part of the Paragraph belongs to another *Stafford.* — I have fince obferved, that *Wood* is not the firft, who hath given us the true Author of the Pamphlet.

The

The juſtly celebrated Mr. *Warton* hath favoured us, in his *Life of* Dr. *Bathurſt*, with ſome *hearſay* particulars concerning *Shakeſpeare* from the papers of *Aubrey*, which had been in the hands of *Wood*; and I ought not to ſuppreſs them, as the *laſt* ſeems to make againſt my doctrine. They came originally, I find, on conſulting the MS. from one Mr. *Beeſton :* and I am ſure Mr. *Warton*, whom I have the honour to call my Friend, and an Aſſociate in the queſtion, will be in no pain about their credit.

" *William Shakeſpeare's* Father was a Butcher, — while he was a Boy he exerciſed his Father's trade, but when he killed a Calf, he would do it in a high ſtile, and make a ſpeech. This *William* being inclined *naturally* to Poetry and Acting, came to *London*, I gueſs, about *eighteen*, and was an Actor in one of the Playhouſes, and did act *exceedingly well.* He began *early* to make Eſſays in dramatique Poetry. — The humour of the *Conſtable* in the *Midſummer Night's Dream* he happen'd to take at *Crendon* k in *Bucks.* — I

k It was obſerved in the former Edition, that this place is not met with in *Spelman's Villare*, or in *Adam's Index*; nor, it might have been added, in the *firſt* and the *laſt* performance of this ſort, *Speed's Tables*, and *Whatley's Gazetteer*: perhaps, however, it may be meant under the name of *Crandon*; — but the inquiry is of no importance. — It ſhould, I think, be written *Credendon*; tho' better Antiquaries than *Aubrey* have acquieſced in the vulgar corruption.

think,

think, I have been told, that he left near three hundred pounds to a *Sifter.* — *He underftood Latin pretty
well,* FOR *he had been in his younger yeares a Schoolmafter
in the Country.*"

: I will be fhort in my animadverfions; and take
them in their order.

The account of the *Trade* of the Family is not
only contrary to all other Tradition, but, as it may
feem, to the inftrument from the Herald's office, fo
frequently reprinted.—— *Shakefpeare* moft certainly
went to *London,* and commenced Actor thro' necef-
fity, not natural inclination. —Nor have we any reafon to fuppofe, that he did act *exceedingly well. Rowe*
tells us from the information of *Betterton,* who was
inquifitive into this point, and had very early opportunities of Inquiry from Sir *W. Davenant,* that
he was no *extraordinary Actor*; and that the top of
his performance was the Ghoft in his own *Hamlet.*
Yet this *Chef d' Oeuvre* did not pleafe : I will give
you an original ftroke at it. Dr. *Lodge,* who was for
ever peftering the town with Pamphlets, publifhed
in the year 1596, *Wits miferie, and the Worlds madneffe, difcovering the Devils incarnat of this Age.* 4to.
One of thefe Devils is *Hate-virtue,* or *Sorrow
for another mans good fucceffe,* who, fays the Doctor,
is " *a foule lubber,* and looks as pale as the Vi-

K 2   fard

fard of the *Ghoft*, which cried fo miferably at the Theatre, like an Oifter-wife, *Hamlet revenge.*" Thus you fee Mr. *Holt's* fuppofed *proof*, in the Appendix to the late Edition, that *Hamlet* was written after 1597, or perhaps 1602, will by no means hold good ; whatever might be the cafe of the particular paffage on which it is founded.

Nor does it appear, that *Shakefpeare* did begin *early* to make *Effays in Dramatique Poetry :* the *Arraignment of Paris*, 1584, which hath fo often been afcribed to him on the credit of *Kirkman* and *Winftanley*,[1] was written by *George Peele*; and *Shakefpeare* is not met with, even as an *Affiftant*, 'till at leaft feven years afterward.[m] — *Nafh* in his Epiftle to the Gentlemen Students of both Univerfities, prefixed to *Greene's Arcadia*, 4to. *black Letter*, recommends his Friend, *Peele*, " as the chiefe fupporter of pleafance now living, the *Atlas* of Poetrie, and *primus Verborum artifex :* whofe firft increafe, the *Arraignment of Paris*, might plead to their

---

[1] Thefe people, who were the *Curls* of the laft age, afcribe likewife to our Author thofe miferable Performances, *Mucidorus*, and the *Merry Devil of Edmonton*.

[m] Mr. *Pope* afferts " The troublefome Raigne of King *John*," in 2 parts, 1611, to have been written by *Shakefpeare* and *Rowley :* — which Edition is a mere Copy of another in *black Letter*, 1591. But I find his affertion is fomewhat to be doubted : for the old Edition hath no name of *Author* at all ; and that of 1611, the Initials only, *W. Sh.* in the Title-page.

opinions

opinions his pregnant dexteritie of wit and manifold
varietie of inuention." [n]

In the next place, unfortunately, there is neither
fuch a Character as a *Conſtable* in the *Midſummer*

[n] *Peele* ſeems to have been taken into the patronage of
the Earl of *Northumberland* about 1593, to whom he de-
dicates in that year, "*The Honour of the Garter*, a Poem
Gratulatorie —— the *Firſtling* confecrated to his noble
name." —— " He was eſteemed, ſays *Anthony Wood*, a
moſt noted Poet, 1579; but when or where he died, I
cannot tell, for *ſo it is*, and always *hath been*, that moſt
POETS die *poor*, and confequently obſcurely, and a hard
matter it is to trace them to their Graves. *Claruit* 1599."
Ath. Oxon. Vol. 1. p. 300.
We had lately in a periodical Pamphlet, called, *The
Theatrical Review*, a very *curious* Letter under the name
of *George Peele*, to one Maſter *Henrie Marle*; relative to a
diſpute between *Shakeſpeare* and *Alleyn*, which was com-
promiſed by *Ben. Jonſon.* —— " I never longed for thy
companye more than laſt night; we were all verie merrie
at the *Globe*, when *Ned Alleyn* did not ſcruple to affyrme
pleaſauntly to thy friende *Will*, that he had ſtolen hys
ſpeeche about the excellencie of acting in *Hamlet* hys
Tragedye, from converſaytions manifold, whych had
paſſed between them, and opinions gyven by *Alleyn*
touchyng that ſubjecte. *Shakeſpeare* did not take this talk
in good ſorte; but *Jonſon* did put an end to the ſtryfe
wyth wittielie ſaying, thys affaire needeth no conten-
tione: you ſtole it from *Ned* no doubte: do not marvel:
haue you not ſeene hym acte tymes out of number? ——
This is pretended to be printed from the original MS.
dated 1600; which agrees well enough with *Wood's Claruit:* but unluckily, *Peele* was dead at leaſt two years before. " As *Anacreon* died by the *Pot*, ſays *Meres*, ſo
George Peele by the *Pox*." *Wit's Treaſury*, 1598. p. 286.

Night's

Night's Dream: nor was the *three hundred pounds* Legacy to a Sifter, but a Daughter.

And to clofe the whole, it is not poffible, according to *Aubrey* himfelf, that *Shakefpeare* could have been fome *years a Schoolmafter in the Country*, : on which circumftance only the fuppofition of his learning is profeffedly founded. He was not furely *very young*, when he was employed to *kill Calves*, and he commenced Player about *Lighteen !* — The truth is, that he left his Father, for a Wife, a year fooner ; and had at leaft two Children born at *Stratford* before he retired from thence to *London*. It is therefore fufficiently clear, that poor *Anthony* had too much reafon for his character of *Aubrey :* You will find it in his own Account of his Life, publifhed by *Hearne,* which I would earneftly recommend to any Hypochondriack ;

" A pretender to Antiquities, roving, magotie-headed, and fometimes little better than crafed : and being exceedingly credulous, would ftuff his many Letters fent to A. W. with *follaries* and mifinformations." p. 577.

Thus much for the Learning of *Shakefpeare* with refpect to the ancient languages : indulge me with an obfervation or two on his fuppofed knowledge of the modern ones, and I will promife to releafe you.

" It is *evident,* we have been told, that he was not unacquainted with the *Italian :*" but let us inquire into the *Evidence.*

Certainly

· Certainly fome *Italian* words and phrafes appear in the Works of *Shakefpeare*; yet if we had nothing elfe to obferve, their Orthography might lead us to fufpect them to be not of the *Writer's* importation. But we can go further, aud prove this.

When *Piftol* " chears up himfelf with ends of verfe," he is only a copy of *Hanniball Gonfaga*, who ranted on yielding himfelf a Prifoner to an *Englifh* Captain in the *Low Countries*, as you may read in an old Collection of Tales, called *Wits, Fits, and Fancies*, o'

" Si Fortuna me tormenta,
Il fperanza me contenta."

And Sir *Richard Hawkins*, in his Voyage to the South-Sea, 1593, throws out the fame jingling Diftich on the lofs of his Pinnace.

" Mafter *Page*, fit ; good Mafter *Page*, fit ; *Preface*. What you want in meat, we'll have in drink," fays Juftice *Shallow's Fac totum, Davy*, in the 2d Part of *Henry* the 4th.

Proface, Sir *Thomas Hanmer* obferves to be *Italian* from *profaccia, much good may it do you.* Mr. *Johnfon* rather thinks it a miftake for *perforce.* Sir *Thomas*

---

o By one *Anthony Copley*, 4to. *black Letter*, it feems to have had many Editions : perhaps the laft was in 1614. — The firft piece of this fort, that I have met with, was printed by *T. Berthelet*, tho' not mention'd by *Ames*, called, " Tales, and quicke anfweres very mery and pleafant to rede." 4to. no date.

however is right; yet it is no argument for his Author's *Italian* knowledge.

Old *Heywood*, the Epigrammatift, addreffed his
Readers long before,

" Readers, reade this thus : for Preface, *Proface*,
Much good do it you, the poore repaft here, &c."

Woerkes. Lond. 4to. 1562.

And *Dekker* in his Play, *If it be not good, the Diuel
is in it,* (which is certainly true, for it is full of
Devils) makes *Shackle-foule,* in the character of *Friar
Rufh,* tempt his Brethren with " choice of difhes"

" To which *proface* ; with blythe lookes fit yee."

Nor hath it efcaped the quibbling manner of the
Water-poet, in the title of a Poem prefixed to his
Praife of Hempfeed, " A Preamble, Preatrot, Prea-
gallop, Preapace, or Preface; and *Proface,* my
Mafters, if your Stomacks ferve."

But the Editors are not contented without coining
Italian. " *Rivo, fays the Drunkard,*" is an Expreffion
of the *madcap* prince of *Wales* ; which Sir *Thomas
Hanmer* corrects to *Ribi, Drink away,* or *again,* as
it fhould rather be tranflated. Dr. *Warburton* accedes
to this; and Mr. *Johnfon* hath admitted it into his
Text; but with an obfervation, that *Rivo* might
poffibly be the cant of *Englifh* Taverns. And fo indeed it was : it occurs frequently in *Marfton.* Take
a quotation from his Comedy of *What you will*; 1607.

" Muficke,

" Muſicke, Tobacco, Sacke, and Sleepe,
The Tide of Sorrow backward keep :
If thou art ſad at others fate,
Rivo, drink deep, give care the mate."

In *Love's Labour loſt*, *Boyet* calls Don *Armado*,

———— " A Spaniard that keeps here in Court,
A Phantaſme, a *Monarcho*." ——

Here too Sir *Thomas* is willing to palm *Italian* upon us. We ſhould read, it ſeems, *Mammuccio*, a Mammet, or Puppet : Ital. *Mammuccia*. But the alluſion is to a fantaſtical *Character* of the time. — " Popular applauſe, ſays *Meres*, dooth nouriſh ſome, neither do they gape after any other thing, but vaine praiſe and glorie, — as in our age *Peter Shakerlye* of *Paules*, and MONARCHO that liued about the Court." p. 178.

I fancy, you will be ſatisfied with one more inſtance.

" *Baccare*, You are marvellous forward, quoth *Gremio* to *Petruchio* in the *Taming of the Shrew*.

" But not ſo *forward*, ſays Mr. *Theobald*, as our Editors are *indolent*. This is a ſtupid corruption of the preſs, that none of them have dived into. We muſt read *Baccalare*, as Mr. *Warburton* acutely obſerved to me, by which the *Italians* mean, Thou ignorant, preſumptuous Man." — " Properly indeed, adds Mr. *Heath*, a *graduated* Scholar, but ironically and ſarcaſtically, a *pretender* to Scholarſhip."

This is admitted by the Editors and Criticks of

L every

every Denomination. Yet the word is neither wrong, nor *Italian :* it was an old proverbial one, ufed frequently by *John Heywood*; who hath made, what he pleafes to call, *Epigrams* upon it.

Take two of them, fuch as they are,

* " *Backare,* quoth *Mortimer* to his Sow :
  Went that Sow *backe* at that biddyng trowe you ?"
  " *Backare,* quoth *Mortimer* to his fow : fe
  Mortimers fow fpeakth as good *latin* as he."

Howel takes this from *Heywood*, in his *Old Sawes and Adages :* and *Philpct* introduces it into the Proverbs collected by *Camden*.

We have but few obfervations concerning *Shakefpeare's* knowledge of the *Spanifh* tongue. Dr. *Grey* indeed is willing to fuppofe, that the Plot of *Romeo and Juliet* may be borrowed from a COMEDY of *Lopes de Vega*. But the *Spaniard*, who was certainly acquainted with *Bandello*, hath not only changed the Cataftrophe, but the names of the Characters. Neither *Romeo* nor *Juliet* ; neither *Montague* nor *Capulet* appears in this performance : and how came they to the knowledge of *Shakefpeare ?* — Nothing is more certain, than that he chiefly followed the Tranflation by *Painter* from the *French* of *Boifteau*, and hence arife the Deviations from *Bandello's* original *Italian*. P

It

P It is remarked, that " *Paris*, tho' in one place called *Earl*, is moft commonly ftiled the *Countie* in this Play.
Shake-

It feems however from a paffage in *Ames's* Typographical Antiquities, that *Painter* was not the only Tranflator of this popular Story : and it is poffible therefore, that *Shakefpeare* might have other affiftance.

In the Induction to the *Taming of the Shrew*, the Tinker attempts to talk *Spanifh :* and *confequently* the Author himfelf was acquainted with it,

" *Paucus pallabris,* let the World flide, *Seffa.*"

But this is a burlefque on *Hieronymo ;* the piece of Bombaft, that I have mentioned to you before :

Shakefpeare feems to have preferred, for fome reafon or other, the *Italian Conte* to our *Count :*—perhaps he took it from the old *Englifh* Novel, from which he is faid to have taken his Plot." — He certainly did fo : *Paris* is there firft ftiled *a young Earle,* and afterward *Counte, Countee,* and *County ;* according to the unfettled Orthography of the time.

The word however is frequently met with in other Writers ; particularly in *Fairfax :*

" As when a Captaine doth befiege fome hold,
   Set in a marifh or high on a hill,
And trieth waies and wiles a thoufand fold,
   To bring the piece fubjected to his will ;
 So far'd the *Countie* with the Pagan bold. &c."

Godfrey of Bulloigne. Book 7. St. 90.

" *Fairfax,* fays Mr. *Hume,* hath tranflated *Taffo* with an elegance and eafe, and at the fame time with an exactnefs, which for that age are furprifing. Each line in the original is faithfully rendered by a correfpondent line in the tranflation." The former part of this character is extremely true ; but the latter not quite fo. In the *Book* above-quoted *Taffo* and *Fairfax* do not even agree in the Number of *Stanza's.*

L 2

" What

" What new device have they devifed, trow ?
Pocas pallabras, &c. ———

Mr. *Whalley* tells us, " the Author of this piece hath the happinefs to be at this time unknown, the remembrance of him having perifhed with himfelf :" *Philips* and others afcribe it to one *William Smith :* but I take this opportunity of informing him, that it was written by *Thomas Kyd*; if he will accept the authority of his Contemporary, *Heywood.*

More hath been faid concerning *Shakefpeare's* acquaintance with the *French* language. In the Play of *Henry the fifth*, we have a whole Scene in it : and in other places it occurs familiarly in the Dialogue.

We may obferve in general, that the early Editions have not half the quantity ; and every fentence, or rather every word moft ridiculoufly blundered. Thefe, for feveral reafons, could not poffibly be publifhed by the Author ; q and it is extremely probable,

that

q Every writer on *Shakefpeare* hath expreffed his aftonifhment, that his author was not folicitous to fecure his Fame by a correct Edition of his performances. This matter is not underftood. When a Poet was connected with a particular Playhoufe, he conftantly fold his Works to the *Company*, and it was their intereft to keep them from a number of Rivals. A favourite Piece, as *Heywood* informs us, only got into print, when it was copied *by the ear*, " for a double fale would bring on a fupicion of honeftie." *Shakefpeare* therefore himfelf publifhed nothing in the *Drama :* when he left the Stage, his copies remained

that the *French* ribaldry was at firſt inſerted by a different hand, ás the many additions moſt certainly
were after he had left the Stage. —— Indeed, every
friend

mained with his Fellow-Managers, *Heminge* and *Condell*;
who at their own retirement, about ſeven years after the
death of the Author, gave the world the Edition now
known by the name of the *firſt Folio*; and call the previous publications " ſtolne and ſurreptitious, maimed
and deformed by the frauds and ſtealths of injurious im-
poſtors." But *this* was printed from the Playhouſe Copies;
which in a ſeries of years had been frequently altered
thro' convenience, caprice, or ignorance. We have a
ſufficient inſtance of the liberties taken by the Actors,
in an old pamphlet, by *Naſh*, called *Lenten Stuffe*,
with the Prayſe of the red Herring, 4to. 1599. where he
aſſures us, that in a Play of his, called the *Iſle of Dogs*,
" *foure acts*, without his conſent, or the leaſt gueſſe of
his drift or ſcope, were ſupplied by the Players."

This however was not his firſt quarrel with them. In
the Epiſtle prefixed to *Greene's Arcadia*, which I have
quoted before, *Tom.* hath a laſh at ſome " vaine glorious
Tragedians," and very plainly at *Shakeſpeare* in particular; which will ſerve for an anſwer to an obſervation of
Mr. *Pope*, that had almoſt been forgotten : " It was
thought a praiſe to *Shakeſpeare*, that he ſcarce ever blot-
ted a line : — I believe the common opinion of his want
of learning proceeded from no better ground. This too
might be thought a *praiſe* by ſome." —— But hear *Naſh*,
who was far from *praiſing :* " I leaue all theſe to the mer-
cy of their *Mother-tongue*, that feed on nought but the
crums that fall from the *Tranſlator's* trencher. —— That
could ſcarcely *Latinize* their neck verſe if they ſhould
haue neede, yet *Engliſh Seneca* read by Candlelight yeelds
many good ſentences —— hee will affoord you whole
Hamlets, I ſhould ſay, *Handfuls* of tragicall ſpeeches."

6   — I

friend to his memory will not eafily believe, that he was acquainted with the Scene between *Catharine* and the *old Gentlewoman* ; or furely he would not have admitted fuch obfcenity and nonfenfe.

Mr. *Hawkins*, in the Appendix to Mr. *Johnfon's* Edition, hath an ingenious obfervation to prove, that *Shakefpeare*, fuppofing the *French* to be his, had very little knowledge of the language.

" Eft-il impoffible d'efchapper la force de ton *Bras ?*" fays a *Frenchman.*—" *Brafs*, cur ?" replies *Piftol.*

—I cannot determine exactly when this *Epiftle* was firft publifhed; but, I fancy, it will carry the original *Hamlet* fomewhat further back than we have hitherto done : and it may be obferved, that the oldeft Copy now extant is faid to be " Enlarged to almoft as much againe as it was." *Gabriel Harvey* printed at the end of the year 1592, " Foure Letters and certaine Sonnetts, efpecially touching *Robert Greene :*" in one of which his *Arcadia* is mentioned.   Now *Nafh's* Epiftle muft have been previous to thefe, as *Gabriel* is quoted in it with applaufe ; and the *Foure Letters* were the beginning of a quarrel.   *Nafh* replied, in " Strange newes of the intercepting certaine Letters, and a Convoy of Verfes, as they were going *privilie* to victuall the *Low Countries*, 1593." *Harvey* rejoined the fame year in " *Pierce's* Supererogation, or a new praife of the old Affe." And *Nafh* again, in " Have with you to *Saffron-walden*, or *Gabriell Harvey's* hunt is up ; containing a full anfwer to the eldeft Sonne of the halter-maker. 1596."

Dr. *Lodge* calls *Nafh* our *true Englifh Aretine :* and *John Taylor*, in his *Kickfey Winfey, or a Lerry Come-twang*, even makes an oath " by fweet Satyricke *Nafh* his urne." — He died before 1606, as appears from an old Comedy, called, " The return from *Parnaffus.*"

" Almoft

. " Almoſt any one knows, that the French word *Bras* is pronounced *Brau*; and what reſemblance of ſound does this bear to *Braſs?*" —

Mr. *Johnſon* makes a doubt, whether the pronunciation of the French language may not be changed, ſince *Shakeſpeare's* time, " if not, ſays he, it may be ſuſpected that ſome other man wrote the *French* ſcenes:" but this does not appear to be the caſe, at leaſt in this termination, from the rules of the Grammarians, or the practice of the Poets. I am certain of the former from the *French Alphabeth* of *De la Mothe*, [r] and the *Orthoepia Gallica* of *John Eliot*; [s] and of the latter from the Rhymes of *Marot*, *Ronſard*, and *Du Bartas*. — Connections of this kind were very common. *Shakeſpeare* himſelf aſſiſted *Ben. Jonſon* in his *Sejanus*, as it was originally written; and *Fletcher* in his *Two noble Kinſmen*.

But what if the *French* ſcene were occaſionally introduced into every Play on this Subject? and per-

---

[r] *Lond.* 1592. 8vo.

[s] *Lond.* 1593. 4to. *Eliot* is almoſt the only *witty* Grammarian, that I have had the fortune to meet with. In his Epiſtle prefatory to the *Gentle Doctors of Gaule*, he cries out for perſecution, very like *Jack* in that moſt poignant of Satires, the *Tale of a Tub*, " I pray you be readie quickly to cauill at my booke, I beſeech you heartily calumniate my doings with ſpeede, I requeſt you humbly controll my method as ſoone as you may, I earneſtly entreat you hiſſe at my inventions, &c."

haps

haps there were more than one before our Poet's. —
In *Pierce Penileffe his Supplication to the Diuell*, 4to.
1592. (which, it feems, from the Epiftle to the Printer,
was not the firft Edition,) the Author, *Nafh*, exclaims,
" What a glorious thing it is to have *Henry the fifth*
reprefented on the Stage leading the *French King*
prifoner, and forcing both him and the *Dolphin* to
fweare fealty !" — And it appears from the Jefts of
the famous Comedian, *Tarlton*, 4to. 1611. that he
had been particularly celebrated in the Part of the
Clown in *Henry the fifth*; but no fuch Character
exifts in the Play of *Shakefpeare*. —— *Henry the
fixth* hath ever been doubted; and a paffage in
the above-quoted piece of *Nafh* may give us reafon to believe, it was previous to our Author.
" How would it haue joyed braue *Talbot* (the
terror of the *French*) to thinke that after he had lyen
two hundred yeare in his Toomb, he fhould triumph
again on the Stage; and haue his bones new em-
balmed with the teares of ten thoufand fpectators at
leaft (at feuerall times) who in the Tragedian that
reprefents his perfon, imagine they behold him frefh
bleeding." ——I haue no doubt but *Henry the fixth*
had the fame Author with *Edward the third*, which
hath been recovered to the world in Mr. *Capell's
Prolufions*.

It hath been obferved, that the *Giant* of *Rabelais*
is

is fometimes alluded to by *Shakefpeare:* and in *his* time no tranflation was extant. — But the Story was in every one's hand.

In a Letter by one *Laneham,* or *Langham,* for the name is written differently, [t] concerning the Entertainment at *Killingwoorth Caflle,* printed 1575, we have a lift of the vulgar Romances of the age, "King *Arthurz* book, *Huon* of *Burdeaus,* Friar *Rous, Howleglafs,* and GARGANTUA. *Meres*[u] mentions him as equally hurtful to young minds with the *Four Sons* of *Aymon,* and the *Seven Champicns.* And *John Taylor*

***

[t] It is indeed of no importance, but I fufpeft the former to be right, as I find it corrupted afterward to *Lanam* and *Lanum.*

[u] This Author by a pleafant miftake in fome fenfible *Conjeftures on Shakefpeare* lately printed at *Oxford,* is quoted by the name of *Maifter.* Perhaps the Title-page was imperfeft; it runs thus " Palladis Tamia. Wits Treafury. Being the fecond part of Wits Common-wealth, By *Francis Meres Maifter* of Artes of both Univerfities."

I am glad out of gratitude to this man, who hath been of frequent fervice to me, that I am enabled to perfeft *Wood's* account of him ; from the affiftance of our *Mafter's* very accurate Lift of Graduates, (which it would do honour to the Univerfity to print at the publick expenfe) and the kind information of a Friend from the Regifter of his Parifh : — He was originally of *Pembroke-Hall,* B. A. in 1587, and M. A. 1591. About 1602 he became Reftor of *Wing* in *Rutland;* and died there, 1646, in the 81ft year of his Age.

M   hath

hath him likewife in his catalogue of *Authors*, prefixed to Sir *Gregory Nonfence*. x

But to come to a conclufion, I will give you an
irrefragable argument, that *Shakefpeare* did *not* un-
derftand *two* very common words in the *French* and
Latin languages.

According to the Articles of agreement between
the Conqueror *Henry* and the King of *France*, the
latter was to ftile the former, (in the correçted *French*
of the modern Editions,) " Noftre *tres cher* filz
Henry Roy d' *Angleterre*; and in *Latin*, *Præclariffimus*
Filius, &c." What, fays Dr. *Warburton*, is *tres cher*
in *French*, *præclariffimus* in *Latin!* we fhould read
præcariffimus. — This appears to be exceedingly true;
but how came the blunder? it is a typographical one

---

x I have quoted many pieces of *John Taylor*, but it was
impoffible to give their original dates. He may be traced
as an Author for more than half a Century. His *Works*
were collected in *Folio*, 1630. but many were printed
afterward; I will mention one for the Humour of the
Title. " Drinke and welcome, or the famous Hiftory of
the moft part of Drinkes in ufe in *Greate Britain* and *Ire-
land*; with an efpecial Declaration of the Potency, Vertue, and Operation of our *Englifh* Ale : with a defcription
of all forts of *Waters*, from the *Ocean Sea* to the *Tears of
a Woman*. 4to. 1633." —— In *Wits Merriment, or Lufty
Drollery*, 1656. we have an " Epitaph on *John Taylor*,
who was born in the City of *Glocefter*, and died in *Phæ-
nix Alley*, in the 75 yeare of his age; you may find him,
if the worms have not devoured him, in *Covent Garden
Church-yard*." p. 130.— He died about two years before.

in *Holingfhed*, which *Shakefpeare* copied; but muft indifputably have corrected, had he been acquainted
with the languages. — " Our faid Father, during his
life, fhall name, call, and write us in *French* in this
maner: Noftre *tres chier* filz., *Henry* Roy d'*Engleterre*
— and in *Latine* in this maner, *Præclariffimus* filius
nofter." Edit 1587. p. 574.

To corroborate this inftance, let me obferve to
you, though it be nothing further to the purpofe,
that another error of the fame kind hath been the
fource of a miftake in an hiftorical paffage of our
Author; which hath ridiculoufly troubled the Criticks.

Richard the third y harangues his army before the
Battle of *Bofworth*,

" Remember

y Some inquiry hath been made for the firft Performers
of the capital Characters in *Shakefpeare*.
We learn, that *Burbage*, the *alter Rofcius* of *Camden*,
was the original *Richard*, from a paffage in the Poems of
Bifhop *Corbet*; who introduces his Hoft at *Bofworth* de-
fcribing the Battle,
" But when he would have faid King *Richard* died,
And call'd *a Horfe, a Horfe*, he *Burbage* cried."
The Play on this fubject mentioned by Sir *John Har-
rington* in his *Apologie for Poetrie*, 1591, and fometimes
miftaken for *Shakefpeare's*, was a *Latin* one, written by
Dr. *Legge*; and acted at *St. John's* in our Univerfity,
fome years before 1588, the date of the Copy in the
Mufeum. This appears from a better MS. in our Library
at *Emmanuel*, with the names of the original Performers.
It is evident from a paffage in *Camden's Annals*, that
there was an old Play likewife on the fubject of *Richard*

the

" Remember whom ye are to cope withal,
A fort of vagabonds, of rafcals, runaways —
And who doth lead them but a paltry fellow
Long kept in *Britaine* at *our Mother's* coft,
A milkfop, &c." ——

" *Our* Mother," Mr. *Theobald* perceives to be
wrong, and *Henry* was fomewhere fecreted on the
Continent: he reads therefore, and all the Editors
after him,

" Long kept in *Bretagne* at *his* mother's coft."

But give me leave to tranfcribe a few more lines
from *Holingfhed,* and you will find at once, that
Shakefpeare had been there before me : —— " Ye fee
further, how a companie of traitors, theeves, out-
laws and runnagates be aiders and partakers of his
feat and enterprife. — And to begin with the erle of
Richmond captaine of this rebellion, he is a Welfh
milkfop — brought up by *my Mother's* meanes and
mine, like a captive in a clofe cage in the court of
Francis duke of *Britaine.*" p. 756.

Holingfhed copies this *verbatim* from his Brother
Chronicler *Hall,* Edit. 1548. *fol.* 54. but his Printer

the fecond ; but I know not in what language. Sir *Gelley
Merrick,* who was concerned in the harebrained bufinefs
of the Earl of *Effex,* and was hanged for it with the ingenious *Cuffe* in 1601, is accufed amongft other things,
" quod *exoletam* Tragœdiam de tragicâ abdicatione Re-
gis *Ricardi fecundi* in publico Theatro coram Conjuratis
datâ pecuniâ agi curaffet."

hath

hath given us by accident the word *Moother* inftead of *Brother*; as it is in the Original, and ought to be in *Shakefpeare*. [z]

I hope, my good Friend, you have by this time acquitted our great Poet of all piratical depredations on the Ancients, and are ready to receive my *Con-clufion.* — He remembered perhaps enough of his *fchool-boy* learning to put the *Hig, hag, hog,* into the mouth of Sir *Hugh Evans*; and might pick up in the Writers of the time, [a] or the courfe of his con-verfation

[z] I cannot take my leave of *H.lingfhed* without clearing up a difficulty, which hath puzzled his Biographers. *Nicholfon* and other Writers have *fuppofed* him a *Clergyman*. *Tanner* goes further, and tells us, that he was educated at *Cambridge*, and actually took the Degree of M. A. in 1544. —— Yet it appears by his Will, printed by *Hearne,* that at the end of life he was only a *Steward*, or a *Ser-vant* in fome capacity or other, to *Thomas Burdett* Efq; of *Bromcote* in *Warwickfhire*. — Thefe things Dr. *Camp-bell* could not reconcile. The truth is, we have no claim to the education of the *Chronicler :* the M. A. in 1544, was not *Raphael*, but one *Ottiwell Holingfhed*, who was afterward named by the Founder one of the firft Fellows of *Trinity College*.

[a] *Afcham* in the Epiftle prefixed to his *Toxophilus*, 1571, obferves of them, that " Manye *Englifhe* writers, ufinge ftraunge wordes, as *Lattine*, *Frenche*, and *Italian*, do make all thinges darke and harde. Ones, fays he, I communed with a man which reafoned the *Englifhe* tongue to be en-riched and encreafet thereby, fayinge : Who will not prayfe that feaft, where a man fhall drincke at a dinner both wyne, ale, and beere ? Truly (quoth I) they be
al

verfation a familiar phrafe or two of *French* or *Italian*: but his *Studies* were moft demonftratively confined to *Nature* and *his own Language.*

In the courfe of this difquifition, you have often fmiled at " all fuch reading, as was never read:" and poffibly I may have indulged it too far: but it is the reading neceffary for a Comment on *Shakefpeare.* Thofe who apply folely to the Ancients for this pur-pofe, may with equal wifdom ftudy the TALMUD for an Expofition of TRISTRAM SHANDY. Nothing but an intimate acquaintance with the Writers of the time, who are frequently of no other value, can point out his allufions, and afcertain his Phrafeology. The Reformers of his Text are for ever equally po-fitive, and equally wrong. The Cant of the Age, a provincial Expreffion, an obfcure Proverb, an obfo-lete Cuftom, a Hint at a Perfon or a Fact no longer remembered, hath continually defeated the beft of our *Gueffers:* You muft not fuppofe me to fpeak at random, when I affure you, that from fome forgot-ten book or other, I can demonftrate this to you in many hundred Places; and I almoft wifh, that I had not been perfuaded into a different Employment.

al good, euery one taken by himfelfe alone, but if you put Malmefye, and facke, redde wyne and white, ale and beere, and al in one pot, you fhall make a drinke neither eafye to be knowen, nor yet holfome for the bodye."

Tho'

Tho' I have as much of the *Natale Solum* about me, as any man whatfoever; yet, I own, the *Primrofe Path* is ftill more pleafing than the *Foffe* or the *Watling Street* :

" Age cannot wither it, nor cuftom ftale
It's infinite variety." ——

And when I am fairly rid of the Duft of topographical Antiquity, which hath continued much longer about me than I expected; you may very probably be troubled again with the ever fruitful Subject of SHAKESPEARE and his COMMENTATORS.

F I N I S.